Cain is on the run. He's about to lay his egg, which means handing it over to his king and never seeing it again. He's wanted to be a father for too long, though, and he's ready to do anything to keep his baby.

Hogan isn't what people would call a friendly person. He's growly and snappish, but only when it comes to those he doesn't like—which is most of the Ogorth clan. When he punches yet another dragon, he's sent off to patrol the forest around the palace, and he stumbles on Cain.

Cain had no idea he was in Ogorth clan territory, but he's relieved he won't have to lay his egg alone. He doesn't expect to find a home with the Ogorth clan, or with Hogan.

Life is good as Cain and Hogan grow closer, but Cain's old clan finds out where he is, and they demand him and his egg back. Will the queen keep her promise to keep him and his baby safe, or will the dangers to her clan be enough for her to give in? Will Cain lose everything he gained and never thought he would have, or does he have a chance to keep living his dreams?

Black Savior

ISBN: 978-1-4874-3234-8
Cover art by Angela Waters

Published by eXtasy Books Inc or
Devine Destinies, an imprint of eXtasy Books Inc

Look for us online at:
www.eXtasybooks.com or www.devinedestinies.com

Black Savior
Ogorth Clan 3

By

Catherine Lievens

Chapter One

Cain pressed his hand to his stomach and swallowed. He waited for the sound of voices to fade before peeking around the corner. The hallway was empty, and he hoped it would stay that way until he passed by. The last thing he needed was for someone to catch him while he tried to sneak out.

Taking the next step was terrifying. He had to do this, but he knew what would happen if he was caught. The clan wouldn't take it well if they found out he was trying to steal one of their babies—as they said. Cain almost snorted, but he needed to stay silent. How could he steal a baby when he was still carrying the egg? This baby was his, not the clan's, and he would make sure they would have a better life than he had, even though it meant leaving the Eiloren clan and everything he'd ever known behind.

He needed to move before someone came back. He was in his human form, hoping it would help him go unnoticed, but it would make it harder for him to run away once he was outside. He had no choice, though. His dragon form was too big, especially now that he was carrying the egg and was close to the time of the laying.

Taking one last deep breath, he snuck around the corner. The hallway was still empty, and he could see the door at the end of it. He was almost there, and with every breath he took, he expected someone to catch him.

No one did.

He reached the door, and with a trembling hand, he

unlocked it and pushed it open. The lock was big, since it was meant to be opened by dragons, and he only had to push it a bit to pass through. He even managed to close it behind himself, although there was nothing he could do about the lock. He didn't even care. He was out, and he was free, or he would be soon, anyway.

First, he had to put more distance between himself and the clan.

He ran like he'd never run before, and that wasn't just a saying. He usually spent most of his time in his dragon form, just like every dragon shifter he knew. Tonight, though, he needed to stay in his human form. It would make it easier for him to hide, which he sorely needed. Eventually, the clan would realize he was gone, and they would come after him. He didn't know how long it would take, but it *would* happen. The clan needed the baby he was carrying, and they would do everything they could to get their hands on the egg. They wouldn't stop for anything, just like he wouldn't let anything stop him from protecting it and keeping it with him.

He didn't know how long he ran. He couldn't hear anyone coming after him, but that didn't stop him. He had to get out of clan territory, but he had no idea where he was going. He'd never been allowed to leave the clan before. He didn't know what life looked like outside of it, not even the forest around it. Even when he was allowed to fly, he always had to stay close by. Now, he didn't know where to go.

Anywhere was better than staying with the clan.

So Cain ran. He ran until he was out of breath and the back of his throat tasted like blood. He ran until he felt like he was going to throw up. His stomach hurt, and he tried to convince himself it was because of the running, but he knew better, even though this was the first egg he would be laying. He'd been taught what to expect when he'd found out he was pregnant, and he knew what his pain meant.

That scared him more than anything else. He couldn't stop to lay the egg, not when he didn't have a safe place to stay and the clan could find him at any moment. He didn't know what he would do now that he had to survive on his own with his baby, but whatever his future would be like was better than giving the baby up as everyone expected him to, including the baby's second father. The baby only had Cain, and Cain would make sure to live up to that. That meant he had to find a safe place where he could lay the egg without the clan finding him, and he hoped he would be able to. If they caught him, they wouldn't hesitate to take the egg away, and he wouldn't be able to do anything. His life and his baby's depended on him being strong enough to make it on his own, and he would.

He had to.

Hogan didn't want to leave the palace. He'd made sure everyone knew about it, but unfortunately for him, it hadn't helped. *Just because I hate that guy doesn't mean I should be punished,* he grumbled.

Octavia sounded amused. *Is that what Morven is doing?*

Why else would he send me to patrol the forest? We both know there's no one out there. The cameras would have picked it up. He's even sending me alone, which means it's a punishment.

Hogan could hear the smile in Octavia's voice. *Maybe you shouldn't have hit that guy, then.*

He was badmouthing Morven and Sheldon. Would you have stood by and done nothing?

Octavia frowned. *What were they saying?*

Nothing you haven't heard already.

A lot of clan dragons had welcomed Sheldon and Blake, even though they were human. Some hadn't, though, and they always made it known. It made Hogan's paws itch to hit them even harder, but he was already in trouble with Morven.

Why he'd done it didn't matter. He wasn't about to tell Morven, who had clearly wanted to push but had only pointed out that he couldn't have his guards hitting each other, whatever the reason behind it. Hogan disagreed, but he wasn't the boss.

Morven was, and he was sending him on his own to patrol the forest tonight.

Hogan groaned. He was going to have to do this, and nothing he could do or say would get him out of it.

You should probably go. The sooner you get it done, the sooner you'll be back, Octavia said.

I have to patrol until dawn.

Well, Slavin and I will be here when you come back. We can go to breakfast together.

Hogan supposed he should be grateful he had at least that to look forward to. With Morven now being head of security and Orran having moved on to being the prince's tutor, it was only the three of them left. Orran and Morven had found their better half, and they were building a life with them. Even though it was something Hogan knew wouldn't happen to him, he was happy for his friends. He was sad to lose the relationship they'd had until now, but he'd always expected it to happen. It had, albeit faster than he'd thought, and he half wondered if Slavin and Octavia would find someone soon, too.

He opened his wings and stretched them out. *I guess I should go. I'm sure Morven is waiting for me so he can look at me all disappointed before I fly away.*

Octavia chuckled. *He loves you like we all do.*

I'm aware, Hogan grumbled. It was a problem, because if they didn't love him, they wouldn't expect anything from him. As it was, Morven expected him not to hit people, even people who said bad things about his human. How was Hogan supposed not to do that? No one should disrespect Morven, no matter who he decided to spend the rest of his life with.

Hogan left Octavia behind and made his way up to the landing platform. Sure enough, Morven was waiting for him when he got there. He was in his human form, like usual these days. Hogan understood why, but it was still strange to see him that way. It was even stranger to have to shift to be able to talk to him.

Morven arched a brow. His stomach jutted in front of him, but he didn't seem to notice. Maybe he was used to it. "Still not telling me why you hit that dragon?"

Right. Hogan had refused to tell Morven about it. Maybe Morven would understand better if he did, but he would also be sad. Morven loved Sheldon, even though Sheldon was a human, and while Hogan didn't understand it, he didn't have to. As long as Morven had what he wanted and was happy, Hogan was a hundred percent behind him. Every dragon in the clan should be, but that wasn't the case.

He crossed his arms over his chest and looked away. "He annoyed me."

Morven sighed. "You can't hit everyone annoying you."

"I can try."

"I want to help you, Hogan, but I can't when you behave this way."

Hogan scowled. "I don't need you to help me. Now, if you don't have anything else to tell me, I need to go. My boss wants me to patrol the forest around the palace, and he's going to yell at me if I don't obey."

That finally got a smile from Morven. "I'm pretty sure he doesn't care. That's what cameras are for."

"But I need to be punished."

Morven's smile fell a bit. "Not punished, no. I just thought it would be a good idea for you to stay away from the palace and everyone in it for a bit."

So he was afraid Hogan would hit someone else. Hogan

wasn't surprised. Morven knew him well, probably better than anyone but his parents. He knew Hogan was quick to react when someone said something he didn't like, and he'd been trying to change that since Hogan had started training to become part of clan security. It was working, but only partially, and not when it came to Hogan's friends. He had very few of them, and he wouldn't allow anyone to badmouth any of them.

Hogan shrugged. "You're probably right. It'll do me good to be on my own for a bit."

"I'm not so sure that's a good thing anymore. Maybe you shouldn't be alone. Every time you are, you end up in trouble."

"I promise I won't this time." Hogan grinned. "Or did you change your mind? I could stay here and go back to my rooms."

Morven pointed a finger toward the platform. "Go. I'll see you at breakfast."

Hogan sighed, but there would be no changing Morven's mind. He winked at him, then shifted and walked away. He could feel Morven still staring at him, but he didn't turn around. Instead, he opened his wings and took flight.

He'd always loved flying. It gave him freedom, even though he was still part of the clan and couldn't stray too far from the palace. It didn't matter. Right now, he was doing what he enjoyed the most in the world, except maybe spending time with his friends. It would be perfect if he and the others were flying together, but as it was, this was better than nothing.

Octavia told me what happened. Slavin's voice came through Hogan's mind.

Hogan groaned. *Does she always tell you everything?*

I'm pretty sure she does, just like she tells you everything you need to know. There was a pause before Slavin continued. *You know you can't hit every asshole who speaks badly of Sheldon and*

Morven, right?

I can try. And Hogan certainly would. Maybe that way, the assholes would stop doing it.

You're going to end up hitting half the dragons in the clan.

I don't have a problem with that.

Of course you don't. Well, we'll be here waiting for you when you come back. You should probably focus on the job now.

Hogan snorted. *There's nothing out here. The cameras would have picked it up. No, Morven is just punishing me.* Because no matter what he said, this *was* a punishment.

They'd stopped patrolling the forest a while ago when they'd installed cameras all around their territory. If anyone came in, even if it was only a rabbit, they knew about it. Having a bunch of dragons flying around was kind of obvious, and it would give away their palace's position. Cameras did a good job while also being hidden, which was what they'd been looking for.

Hogan flew down until his stomach brushed against the top of the trees. Even though this wasn't necessary, he could admit he'd missed it. It had been one of his first jobs when he'd enrolled with palace security, and it had helped him not get kicked out right away. He'd been tempted to hit assholes even back then, so nothing much had changed.

He sighed. He realized he had to be more careful. A lot of dragons didn't like him, but he'd never cared. He still didn't, not when it came to most of them. The only people he cared about were his parents, Morven, Slavin, Octavia, and Orran. Maybe Sheldon and Blake, too. And of course, the queen, although that was different. He would die to protect those few people, along with Sheldon and Morven's baby. Morven was heavily pregnant, and he shouldn't have to deal with assholes who thought he should be expelled from the clan because of who he loved. What the fuck did they care?

A movement under him caught his eye, and he frowned. It was probably an animal, but there weren't many of them in the forest just under the mountain where the palace was located. They'd learned a long time ago that the palace was full of predators, even though the clan had stopped hunting them a while back. It would take a long time for the forest to be full of animals again, and it was a rare sight to see any of them. Something had moved, though, so Hogan lowered himself until he could take a better look.

It wasn't a rabbit or a deer. It looked like a human, even though Hogan was sure that couldn't be the case. It was dark, but even with his dragon eyes, it was hard for him to see what was going on. Not that it mattered. Someone was in the clan's forest, which meant Hogan had to stop them.

He flew faster, then turned around. As soon as he could, he landed in the middle of the forest, ignoring the way he was scratching his sides and wings against the trees. He stopped in front of the person who was running, and they screeched to a halt, almost stumbling back as they watched him with wide eyes.

Dammit. He couldn't talk to them in this form. He didn't want to shift, but he had no choice. He did it as quickly as possible, then stood there, staring. "Who are you, and what are you doing in my clan's forest?" he growled.

Cain stared at the dragon who had landed in front of him. He was pretty sure it was a male from the voice, but he suspected that wouldn't change anything.

"I'm talking to you. What are you doing here?" the dragon repeated.

Cain swallowed and clutched his stomach. It felt like it was tearing apart, and he didn't know how to deal with it or with this dragon. "I'm sorry," he said, his voice trembling. "I didn't mean to invade another clan's territory."

The dragon continued staring. Cain stared back until he

couldn't. The next contraction folded him in half, and he reached out to hold himself up against the closest tree. He heard the dragon move, and when he looked up once the contraction had faded, the dragon was so close Cain could have touched them.

He wanted to. He wanted to grab the dragon's hand and squeeze during the next contraction. He wanted to have someone with him while he laid his egg. He had no time to explain what was going on. He was pretty sure the egg was about to come out, and he couldn't do that on his feet.

He lowered himself to the ground. Hopefully, this dragon would protect him and his egg if someone attacked. He'd said Cain was in his clan's territory, which meant he wasn't in Eiloren territory anymore. That was a good thing. He could deal with everything else once this was over.

"What are you doing?" the dragon asked.

"I'm about to lay an egg. What do you think I'm doing?" Cain snapped back.

The dragon stared at him for a moment.

Cain dismissed him, focused on getting his baby out of him. The next contraction was already coming, but hopefully, there weren't many of them left.

"You can't do that here," the dragon said. "Didn't you hear me? You're in Ogorth clan territory. You can't stay here."

So that was where Cain had ended up. He hadn't realized he'd run so far, but he was glad he had. The Ogorth clan had a good reputation, even with his old clan. He was hopeful they wouldn't kick his ass out, at least until he was done laying his egg, although from the way this dragon was talking to him, he wasn't entirely sure about that. But there was nothing else to do. The egg wouldn't stay in, and Cain couldn't have it while he was on the run. He had to stop, no matter who was bitching about it.

He breathed through the contraction, clutching his

stomach, and praying it was almost over. He took a deep breath once it had faded, then turned his attention to the dragon. "My name is Cain. I'm sorry for invading your territory, and I'll be gone as soon as I can, but as you probably noticed, I'm about to lay an egg. I'm not going anywhere until it's out of me."

The dragon stared down at him.

The forest had grown a little lighter because the clouds had moved away from the moon, and Cain could see they were a deep black. The dragon's eyes were gorgeous and so very different from Cain's own pale yellow.

"Why aren't you with your clan? Surely they'd help you lay your egg," the dragon said.

Cain shook his head. "I can't allow them to get their hands on it. Please. I ran away, and they'll take my baby from me if they reach me. I won't stay here long, I promise. Just let me do this first." Cain doubted he would be able to run any longer with the pain, but he would try if he had to do it. Hopefully, though, this dragon wouldn't be as cruel as the dragons in his old clan had been.

The dragon looked like he didn't know what to do. He looked from Cain to the forest around them. That allowed Cain to observe him and gave him a distraction from the pain.

The dragon was black, and so was his short hair that glinted in the moonlight. Cain was pretty sure it was a male from his voice, but to be sure, he would have to ask. He wasn't planning on doing that it. He didn't want the dragon to get angry and possibly hit him. It would hurt, even though from what Cain could tell, the dragon was slightly shorter than he was.

The dragon's shoulders relaxed after a few moments. "Fine. You can lay your egg here."

Cain was grateful, since he could feel another contraction coming. He tightened his hold around his stomach and tried to breathe through it. It felt like his stomach was tearing apart, but he knew it was only temporary. He would be fine once the egg was out of his body.

"You don't need help, right?" the dragon asked.

Cade laughed through the end of the contraction. He was pretty sure it made the pain worse, but what could he do? "I wouldn't hate it if you decided to help me."

"I've never done this. I don't know what to do."

"I've never done this, either." He swallowed. "My name is Cain." The dragon stared as if he didn't know what to do. Cain huffed and asked, "What's yours?"

"Why do you want to know?"

"Because you're the only one around here, which means you'll be the only one to help me lay my egg. I'd like to know what to call you while you do so."

Cain wouldn't be doing this alone like he'd expected, but he wasn't sure it was a good thing. The Ogorth clan had a good reputation, but that didn't mean all of its dragons were good. Still, this one had allowed him to stay for now, which was more than he'd expected. If this had been his clan, the dragon would have either dragged him in front of the king or killed him. The Ogorth clan was giving Cain a better opportunity than he ever had with the Eiloren clan, and Cain hoped that would continue.

Then the next contraction gripped his stomach, and he couldn't think of anything else.

Hogan had no idea what to do. He'd never had to help someone lay their egg, and he didn't know where to start. What if he did something wrong? Cain was writhing on the ground, holding his stomach and clearly in pain, and Hogan couldn't remember how to help him.

He knelt next to Cain. He was tempted to take his hand,

but he didn't know how Cain would take it. "My name is Hogan," he said.

Cain breathed in and out, but it still took him a moment to look at Hogan. "Thanks for telling me. Are you male, female, or neither?"

"Male. What about you?"

"Same." He swallowed.

Hogan wanted to push Cain's hair away from his face. Cain was sweating, and the hair clung to his forehead. It was a pale color, maybe yellow, and Hogan wanted to touch it. Instead, he said, "I'll shift and let someone know what's going on."

Before he could get to his feet, Cain's hand shot out, and he grabbed one of his. "Please stay. I don't want to do this alone."

"I don't know how to help you." And it terrified Hogan. He'd never been one to want kids, even though he knew they were a blessing for the clan and the parents. He couldn't imagine himself with a child, and while Cain's wouldn't be his, he was pretty sure he would manage to fuck the kid up if he as much as touched the egg.

Cain shook his head. "It doesn't matter. It's almost over anyway. I just need you to hold my hand. Please."

He was begging, and that sounded wrong coming from his lips. Hogan wanted to shift and call for help more than ever. Instead, he knelt next to Cain, unhooked Cain's hand from his wrist, and linked their fingers together.

Cain was slightly taller than Hogan, but he was much slimmer, and his hand looked small in Hogan's. He was strong, though, and Hogan groaned when Cain squeezed his hand so hard that he was pretty sure he would break it.

"Sorry, sorry, sorry," Cain chanted.

Hogan might never have helped anyone give birth, but he knew how it worked. He'd informed himself when Morven got pregnant, just in case. Cain was working through the contractions, and from the looks and sound of it, they were coming closer and closer and were stronger than ever. He was right—he would be laying his egg soon.

Hogan swallowed. He could remember every word of the books he'd read about laying eggs and birth, and hopefully, it would be enough to help Cain. He had to keep his cool and focus. "You need to let go of me," he said.

Cain shook his head. "I can't. I don't want to."

"I just want to check your pouch."

Cain's eyes snapped open. "Why?"

"To make sure everything is going well."

"You said you didn't know how to do this."

"Not practically, but I know the theory. It's better than nothing, right?"

Cain stared for a moment before nodding. "I suppose it is. Fine. You can check my pouch."

Hogan wiggled his fingers once Cain let them go. Thankfully, nothing was broken, but they hurt a bit. He brushed it off and moved until he was kneeling between Cain's legs. His stomach was so distended that he looked like he was about to explode. That wouldn't be the case, but it still made Hogan uneasy.

He looked at Cain's pouch. It was opening, just like it was supposed to. It was also swollen, and the sight made Hogan shudder in horror. It was too easy to imagine himself in Cain's place, and he never wanted that to happen. No matter what his parents said, there was no way that going through this was a good thing. He didn't know why anyone would want to lay eggs, but he *did* know he never would.

He saw the moment the next contraction hit Cain. Cain threw his head back, and his entire body tightened with pain. Hogan kept his focus on the pouch, watching as it opened slightly more. He could see the egg peek through the opening, and he knew it was almost time. "Just a bit longer," he murmured. He wanted to soothe Cain, so he gently put his hand on Cain's thigh. He didn't know if it worked, but after a moment, Cain's body relaxed.

He was panting, and his body was damp with sweat. "How much longer?" he asked. He sounded exhausted.

"A contraction, maybe two. I promise you're almost done."

Cain nodded and flopped onto the ground. "This isn't how I thought it would go."

"You shouldn't be doing this on your own." Where was the egg's other parent? Cain was running from something, probably his clan, but that didn't explain why he was on his own.

"I'm not. I'm doing this with you."

Hogan opened his mouth to say something, although what, he didn't know. Before one word could pass his lips, Cain's body tensed again. He screamed, and the pouch opened wide enough that the egg moved forward. It wasn't quite enough for it to slip out, but Hogan knew what he needed to do. That was why he'd read those books, after all. He'd wanted to be prepared in case Morven needed him to do this, and he was glad he had.

He reached forward and gently slipped his fingers into the pouch. Cain's body convulsed under him, but Hogan kept his focus on the egg. He slowly slid it out, and Cain's body let go. It was more than ready for the egg to be laid.

Cain slumped on the cold earth, his panting the only sound in the forest. Hogan was holding the egg, and he was staring at it, fascinated. He'd never touched an egg or seen one up close. He hadn't expected to, either. He hadn't been about to ask Morven and Sheldon if he could touch theirs, no matter how much he wanted to. He might not wish to have children himself, but this was incredible.

The egg shone in the moonlight. It was a pale color, just like Cain, and slick with the fluids that had helped the laying. Hogan looked around for something to clean it, but before he could do anything, Cain sat up and took the egg. Hogan let go, and Cain cradled the egg against his chest, looking as if he hadn't slept in a week but also like he was ready to fight Hogan if he needed to. He would defend his baby, and Hogan's heart squeezed at the sight.

Cain shouldn't be this afraid. He shouldn't be doing this on his own or with Hogan, which was basically the same thing.

"I'll be going as soon as I can get to my feet," Cain promised.

The idea alarmed Hogan. "You can't."

"Why? Am I your prisoner?"

Hogan blinked. "Of course not. You've just laid your egg, though. You need rest and food, not to walk around the forest. Do you even know where you are?"

"In Ogorth clan territory. I'm just passing through."

Hogan arched a brow. "And where are you going?"

Cain hesitated, then shrugged. "I don't know. Wherever I can find a safe place to raise my baby."

"Not back to your clan?"

"Never. I'll run away if you contact them."

Whatever the Eiloren clan had done, it had been enough to send Cain running even though he'd known he was about to lay his egg. The thought made Hogan want to find all the clan members and tear them apart with his bare hands, but he had to focus on Cain first. He was an intruder, but Hogan suspected he had a good reason. "I'll take you to the palace," he said.

Cain shook his head. "You can't. Your queen would have to give me back to my clan, and it's not possible. They would take my egg from me, and I would never see it again."

There was the urge to tear apart every single member of the Eiloren clan again. Instead of getting to his feet and flying in that direction, Hogan leaned closer to Cain. He was still kneeling between Cain's legs, and the position was an awkward one. He wanted Cain to trust him, even though he had no idea why. "The queen is a good ruler. She won't give you up if you don't want to go."

Cain's eyes were wide. It was almost as if he was trying very hard to keep them that way so he wouldn't fall asleep. Hogan had done that himself a few times, and he knew how hard it was.

"Why wouldn't she? I'd only bring trouble to your clan," Cain murmured.

"I know. If you need help, though, she'll give it to you. I promise." And if she didn't, Hogan was ready to fight for Cain and his egg.

He didn't know why. It didn't make sense, not when he didn't know Cain. Helping him lay his egg had brought them closer, and Hogan felt responsible. Cain's egg might not be Hogan's, but he'd helped bring it into the world. He'd been there when Cain needed him, and he felt responsible. He realized he couldn't make promises about what the queen would do, but he *could* promise his own behavior.

"Whatever happens, I'll make sure you're safe," he said.

"Even if it goes against your queen's orders?"

"Even then." Hogan was sure she would allow Cain to stay, but he was ready to shoulder this responsibility if she didn't. He'd promised, and he wasn't one to go back on his promises.

CHAPTER TWO

Hogan had probably made a mistake. He should have gone to Morven and the queen right away when he'd arrived back at the palace with Cain, but instead, he'd stashed Cain in his rooms. He didn't know why, and he had no intention of analyzing his feelings. He just knew he wanted to protect Cain, and that included protecting him from anyone who wanted to kick him out of the palace.

But Hogan didn't know if anyone wanted that. They might, but they didn't even know Cain was there. Besides, Hogan wasn't going to be able to hide Cain for long. Cain needed a healer to see him, as well as food. Hogan had brought him something from breakfast, but it wouldn't last for long, and Cain needed more.

That meant Hogan had to talk to someone, and he wasn't looking forward to it. He was used to fucking up, but even this was big for him.

He peered at Cain, who was sleeping in Hogan's nest, hugging his egg. He'd only woken up to eat breakfast, and he'd gone to sleep again right away after that. He clearly needed it after the birth and running away from his clan. Hogan didn't want to wake him up, so he made sure to lock the door when he left. His parents had a key, but hopefully they would stay away from his rooms today. Even if they didn't, they wouldn't say anything before talking to him. Hogan had left a note for Cain in case he woke up before he came back, although, from the looks of it, he doubted that would happen. He suspected Cain would sleep for hours, which hopefully would give Hogan time to fix things and give him good news when he woke up.

Hogan made his way toward Morven's office. Morven was his superior, the head of palace security, and the only person Hogan could talk to about this. He didn't want to, because Morven was heavily pregnant and it couldn't be good for him or the egg, but what choice did he have?

Luckily for him, Morven wasn't in his office when he arrived. Orran was, though, and Hogan remembered that Orran was temporarily helping Morven since Morven was pregnant. His regular job was tutoring the prince, but Blue was only a few months old, so there wasn't much for Orran to do except babysit him when it was needed.

Orran looked up when Hogan knocked on the door. He was in his human form, which again wasn't a surprise, since he was in a relationship with a human. He smiled from behind the small desk, then gestured at Hogan to come in. "Do you want me to shift?" he asked.

Hogan shook his head and shifted to his human form.

Orran arched a brow, but he didn't say anything about it.

Hogan shrugged. "I know you prefer this form these days."

"That doesn't mean you have to use it, too. And it's not that I prefer it. It's just that it's easier this way."

"Blake wouldn't understand you if you stayed in your dragon form."

"Exactly. And I think all of us have been neglecting our human form too much. It was easier to ignore it, but we're shifters for a reason."

Hogan had never thought about that, but maybe Orran had a point. Initially, it had been strange to shift to his human form, but now it was becoming a habit, and he didn't hate it.

"What's going on?" a voice said behind Hogan.

He sighed and turned to face Morven. "Good morning.

How are you feeling?"

Morven's eyes narrowed, and he crossed his arms over his chest. He was holding a cup, and Hogan briefly wondered if he would put it down on his belly. It was big enough to hold it. "What are you doing here?" Morven asked.

Hogan was disappointed when he put the cup down on the desk Orran was sitting behind. It was probably a better idea, though. "I needed to talk to Orran," Hogan said.

Hogan hadn't thought it possible, but Morven's eyes narrowed even more. "You mean you needed to talk to me, don't you? Because I'm your superior, not Orran."

"He's sitting behind your desk."

"Only because he's been helping me. What's going on, Hogan? Are you in trouble again?"

Hogan shuffled his feet. This was awkward, and especially so because he was in his human form. He didn't know how to guard his expression in this form, which was probably why Morven already knew he was in trouble.

Or maybe it was because Hogan was always in some kind of trouble.

"What did you do?" Morven asked slowly.

"I should talk to Orran. You shouldn't be stressed right now."

"So you admit that whatever you're about to say is going to stress me out."

"I'm trying to help you. You're pregnant. You should focus on your egg, not on what I did." Hogan would never forgive himself if something happened to Morven or his baby and it was his fault.

Morven pinched the bridge of his nose and sighed heavily. When he opened his eyes again, he looked more relaxed, although not by much. "As grateful as I am to Orran for helping me, I'm still your superior and the head of security. Whatever is going on, I'm the one who needs to hear it, not him. I'm listening, Hogan."

Hogan sucked in a breath. "Last night, you sent me to the forest."

"Is that what this is about? I know you don't like that kind of job, but no one does. It wasn't a punishment, though, Hogan. I thought you needed to cool down and that this was the best way to make that happen."

"That's not what I was talking about," Hogan rushed to say. Morven shouldn't feel guilty about sending him to the forest.

For one, he was Hogan's superior, and Hogan had done something he shouldn't have. Hogan also wouldn't have met Cain if he hadn't been there, and he shuddered at the thought of what would have happened to him. He would have laid his egg on his own, and once he was done, he would have started running again. That wouldn't have been good for either of them, and Hogan was glad he'd thought to take them to the palace.

"What are you talking about, then?" Morven asked. He sounded cautious, as if he expected something bad to have happened.

Hogan supposed that was the case. "When I was there, I saw something. Someone."

Morven groaned. "Am I going to have to torture it out of you? Just get to the point before I have a heart attack."

Hogan's eyes widened. "I told you I didn't want to stress you out."

Morven waved. "Just go on. I'll be fine."

"Okay. Well, I saw someone. I don't know why the cameras didn't, especially since he's a dragon."

Both Morven and Orran straightened. "A dragon?" Orran asked. "Was it a clan member?"

"No. He was running, and I stopped him. He's from the Eiloren clan, and he's running away from them."

"Explain," Morven snapped.

"He was heavily pregnant when I found him. He gave birth in the forest, and I helped him. He begged me not to contact his clan, and he said he was going to continue running once he was done. I couldn't allow that to happen. He needed rest and to be protected."

"What did you do?" Morven slowly asked.

"I promised him he would be safe, and I intend to keep that promise. That's why I brought him to my rooms."

Morven stared. Hogan tried to look like he was convinced about what he'd done, but he knew he'd made a mistake. He should have talked to Morven right away when he'd found Cain, but Morven had been in bed, and he needed rest, too.

"Are you telling us that you snuck a dragon and his egg inside the palace last night?" Orran asked.

"I did. And I didn't finish my shift in the forest. Sorry."

Orran shook his head. "We'll talk about that later. Why didn't you tell anyone?"

"Cain was freaking out. I believe he thought that if he let me out of his sight, I would go straight to the queen and tell her he was there. He thinks she's going to kick him out. He needs us, though. I don't know what happened with the Eiloren clan exactly, but he said they were going to take away his baby, and that's not right."

Morven looked like his head was about to explode. "You should have told someone. You should have told *me,* since I'm your superior and the head of security. The fact that I'm pregnant doesn't have anything to do with this. It doesn't make me an idiot or incapable of doing my job," he ground out.

Hogan had never wanted Morven to feel like he was judging him for being pregnant. "I know that. But I also know that pregnancy isn't easy, especially in your case. I didn't want to wake you up for this. Besides, Cain has been sleeping since he arrived. He only woke up to have breakfast, then went back to sleep."

"Where is he now?"

"In my rooms."

Orran nodded and got to his feet. "I need to talk to the queen. She'll want to know about this and probably to talk to you."

"And Cain?"

Orran looked amused. "Definitely Cain, too." He hesitated. "I think you made the right choice when you decided to help him. You should have told someone, though."

"I'm aware of it, and I apologize. We need to focus on helping him now. You can punish me all you want once this is over, but he needs to know he can stay and that he'll be safe." Hogan had made a promise, and he tried never to break them.

He needed to do this for Cain, but more importantly, Cain had to be able to relax and know that no one would force him to go back to his old clan.

The room was empty when Cain woke up. He didn't know what to think about that for the first few minutes. Then he saw the note Hogan had left him. He was grateful for it, because it meant he didn't freak out at the thought of being abandoned, or worse, given back to the Eiloren clan. Still, knowing that Hogan was talking to his superior about him made Cain nervous, and it was hard for him not to start pacing the room. He tried to focus on his egg instead, and thankfully, that was fairly easy.

He'd laid his egg. He was a father, even though the baby wasn't out yet. For now, Cain had to keep the egg warm and safe, which was why he stayed in the nest, wrapped around it. Just like he'd thought last night, it was a pale yellow, and it felt smooth but bumpy. He was grateful, even though it didn't mean that his baby would be the same color. The other father was a dark purple, so the baby would probably be a mix of that and yellow.

Cain wrinkled his nose. He didn't want his baby to have any sign of their other father. The man didn't deserve to be a father, not when he'd been so ready to hand over the egg to the clan. He hadn't seen a problem with what they were doing, and he'd refused to help Cain escape. Cain supposed he should be grateful he hadn't run to the king to tell him what Cain was planning. Maybe he had, and Cain didn't know. That was why Cain hadn't told him what he would do in detail and why he'd left as soon as he talked to him.

Cain swallowed. For now, he and his baby were safe, and he hoped that would continue. He had no way to know, though. Hogan had said he would need to talk to his queen, but that didn't mean she would allow Cain to remain here. If she didn't, Cain didn't know what he would do. Leave again, of course, but where would he go? The only place he'd ever known in his life was the Eiloren clan. He'd never been alone, and he'd never had to make this kind of decision. He didn't know if he would be able to, but he supposed he was going to find out.

The sound of a key in the door lock made him sit up. He clutched his egg to his chest, holding his breath. He only released it when Hogan stepped in.

Hogan closed the door behind himself and locked it again. Cain took a moment to peek at him, and just like he'd thought last night, Hogan was gorgeous. He was in his human form now, and he was all muscles and sleek movements. His shoulders were broad and his arms strong. It was too easy to imagine what they would feel like around Cain, so Cain shook his head to get the image out of it.

"You're awake," Hogan said.

Cain straightened and held his egg tighter. "I am."

"Good, because the queen wants to talk to you." Hogan

moved closer and knelt at the edge of the nest. "How's the egg?"

Cain had already realized that for some reason, Hogan was fascinated by his egg. Maybe this clan was like the Eiloren clan and they took the eggs away from the parents as soon as they laid them. He hoped that wasn't the case. If it was, he would have to run away again, and he wasn't looking forward to that. "It's fine."

Hogan nodded. "Did you keep it warm?"

"Of course I did."

Hogan raised his hands. "I was just checking. We don't have a lot of babies here, and I just want to keep it and you safe."

Cain hoped that was the case. He wanted to trust Hogan, but he was still hesitant. Even though Hogan had helped him when he shouldn't have, there was still a chance he would give Cain up. He'd promised he wouldn't, but Cain didn't really know him. He had no way to know if Hogan would keep that promise.

Cain cleared his throat. "You said your queen wants to talk to me?"

Hogan nodded. "I talked to my friend, Morven. Well, in this case, he was my superior, I guess. He was pissed, but the queen seemed more amused than anything about this. I guess she's used to me creating trouble."

"You're a troublemaker?" Cain would never have guessed it, although maybe he should have. Hogan *had* snuck him into the palace, after all.

"Not really. I just don't like people talking badly about my friends. She's waiting for us now, so we should probably head out."

Cain swallowed. "All right." Even though he was terrified, it would be no use for him to waste time. Eventually, he would have to face the queen. He might as well do it now so he'd know what would happen to him.

Cain wanted to shift back to his dragon form. It made him feel less vulnerable, but he wouldn't be able to hold his egg if he did, so he stayed human. Thankfully, Hogan did, too, and together, they left Hogan's rooms.

Cain hadn't seen much of the palace last night when Hogan had snuck him in, but now that he did, he was impressed. The place where the Eiloren clan lived wasn't this big, and from what Cain could see, it was because it didn't have nearly as many members. Cain had no idea how many dragons lived here, but it had to be a lot for the palace to be this big.

"I don't want you to worry," Hogan was saying. "I know that facing the queen is nerve-racking. It doesn't often happen to me, but every time it does, I feel like running away screaming."

He was babbling, which made Cain smile. He hadn't thought Hogan would be that kind of guy, and he found it both fascinating and kind of adorable. He wasn't about to tell Hogan that, but he couldn't help but stare.

"Anyway, she's a good person," Hogan continued. "She's open-minded, and I'm sure she'll understand why you can't go back to the Eiloren clan."

"Understanding it doesn't mean she'll allow me to stay," Cain murmured.

"Maybe not, but I think she will. We even have humans! Why wouldn't she allow you to stay?"

Cain was surprised at the mention of humans, but his situation was different. He knew how his king would have reacted if someone in his situation had begged him to be allowed to stay. He would have shown them the door, although probably not before stealing their egg. If he had to, Cain would leave. He was sure he could find a spot where he could raise his egg on his own. He wasn't looking forward to it, but he'd do it.

"Besides, I'll fight for you," Hogan added.

That made Cain frown. "Why would you? I'm nothing to you. If anything, I owe you."

"I made a promise, and I'll keep it." Hogan stopped in front of two massive doors. "Ready?"

Cain shook his head. "I'm scared."

"I won't tell you that you have nothing to be scared of, but remember, I promised I would take care of you, and I never break my promises."

Cain was pretty sure that was a lie, but he still nodded. Hogan pushed one of the doors open and stepped in. Cain followed him. He swallowed at the sight of the guards lining the throne room. He wasn't surprised by their presence, but it made him even more nervous. Then his gaze stopped on a blue dragon spread out on the throne. It had to be the queen, and he found his steps faltering.

She wasn't alone. Two dragons in their human forms stood by her side, one of them heavily pregnant. Cain couldn't look away from him. This had to be Hogan's friend, the one he'd been afraid to talk to because he didn't want to add to the stress of pregnancy. He was green and tall, and if Cain remembered well, male. The dragon standing next to him was a blue dragon like the queen. Cain briefly wondered if he needed to shift, since the queen was in her dragon form, but thankfully, he didn't have to ask. The queen shifted to her human form and sat on the throne, watching him.

"Welcome," she said.

Cain wanted to run away screaming. Instead, he bowed. "Your Majesty."

"I have to say I'm curious about what's going on. Hogan already mentioned a few things, but I'd like to hear it from you. I'd like to know everything there is to know about the situation before making a decision about whether or not you'll be allowed to stay."

Cain swallowed. "Of course." He prayed that once she knew what was going on, she'd allow him either to stay or to leave without trying to give him back to the Eiloren clan. He didn't know what he would do if that wasn't the case, but he found himself leaning closer to Hogan.

Even though he didn't know Hogan, he trusted him. It didn't make sense, but it didn't have to.

Cain took a deep breath and started speaking.

Hogan already knew parts of what Cain was saying, but he still found himself fighting the urge to leave the palace and go to the Eiloren clan to beat all of them up, especially their king.

"In my clan," Cain slowly explained, "all the eggs have to be handed over to the king and his people as soon as they're laid. They're the ones who take care of the eggs, and parents have nothing to do with the children once they're born. The clan raises them and decides what they will do once they're older. We have no say in it, as parents or as adults. That's what they wanted to do to my egg. They wanted me to hand it over once I laid it, and I would never have seen it again. I wouldn't have met my baby until they were adults, and even then, I wouldn't have known who they were."

The queen was frowning, which Hogan hoped was a good thing in this situation. "Are you saying you never knew your parents?" she asked.

Cain shook his head. "No. Or maybe I did, but I didn't know it was them. There's no way for any of us to know who our parents are. Once the egg is handed over, it's gone." He sucked in a breath. "I couldn't let that happen. That's why I ran away before laying the egg. I'm grateful for the help you and your clan gave me, and if you need me to, I'll be gone in minutes. But please, I beg you. Don't contact the Eiloren clan."

Hogan held his breath. He already knew what he would do

if the queen told Cain that she would do what he'd asked her not to do. It didn't make sense, but he didn't care much about that. He wouldn't hesitate to grab Cain and run away with him if he had to.

The queen leaned back, clearly thinking about what was going on. "Have you seen our healers yet?" she asked.

"No, and I don't expect anything. It was already so much that Hogan helped me lay my egg. I just need a safe place for a few days."

The queen waved. "Don't worry about that. Hogan, make sure he sees the healers once we're done here. I want to be sure both he and his baby are okay." She turned her attention back to Cain. "As for you, I'll allow you to stay with us. That doesn't make you a clan member yet, though. I need some time to think about it, but I want to reassure you that I won't contact the Eiloren clan. If what you're saying is true and they take away the eggs from the parents, it's horrific, and I can't allow them to do that to you. I'm a mother, and I can only imagine what it would have been like if I'd had to hand over my egg once I laid it. You'll be safe here, Cain. So will your baby. Give me a few days to think about all of this, and I'll talk to you again. I want you to think about it, too. Becoming part of our clan will not be easy. We've had problems in the past few years, and you might become part of them once people find out about you. Right now, though, you should focus on your baby."

Hogan was relieved. He'd been ready to argue with the queen that Cain should be allowed to stay, but he wouldn't have to, not yet, anyway. She'd made a point to tell Cain that he wasn't a clan member, but that was okay. For now, Cain didn't need to be one. Hopefully, he would be soon.

The queen was done speaking, and she turned back to Orran. Morven stepped toward Hogan and Cain, gesturing at the door. Hogan didn't waste time moving to it. He put a hand on the small of Cain's back to guide him, while Morven followed them. Thankfully, he stayed silent until they were outside the throne room with the doors closed behind them.

"Welcome to the clan," Morven told Cain. His gaze flickered to Hogan. "So you *really* helped him lay his egg?"

Hogan shrugged. "What did you expect me to do? Watch him while he was doing it?"

"I just didn't think you'd do something like that."

Neither had Hogan, but he felt strangely proud of having done it. There hadn't been much for him to do apart from helping the egg slide out of Cain's body, but he'd been there for Cain when no one else had been, and he knew it had helped.

"I don't know what I would have done if he hadn't been there," Cain murmured. He was still holding his egg to his chest as if he expected someone to snatch it away from him. After what he'd just explained, it made sense.

"Hogan might be grumpy, but he's a good person," Morven said with a smile.

Hogan groaned. "Can we stop talking about me and focus on what's important? I need to get Cain a harness for both his forms so he doesn't have to hold the egg all the time."

The way Morven looked at Hogan was strange and unusual, but Hogan didn't have the time to focus on it. A group of three dragons was coming toward them, and they were all staring at Cain. Hogan moved so he'd be closer to Cain with Morven on Cain's other side, and once the three dragons reached them, he bared his teeth and growled at them. Even though they were in their dragon form, they jumped and scampered away, leaving Hogan smug and satisfied until he remembered that Morven didn't want him growling at people without a good reason. This had been a good reason, though, right? Those dragons had obviously noticed Cain was holding an egg, and they'd been about to talk to him. They might have been rude or something like that.

When Hogan looked at Morven, Morven was smiling. Hogan wanted to ask why, but he was afraid to, so instead he focused on Cain again.

"We can find those harnesses later," Morven said. "In the meantime, Cain, why don't you come to lunch with us? The rest of our little group will already be in the dining room, and you can meet them. Hogan will have to go to work eventually, and I'm sure it will do you good to have other friendly people to be with. I can only imagine how disorienting being with a new clan is to you, especially after just laying your egg."

"Thank you," Cain said. His voice was soft, but he sounded more relaxed than he'd been since Hogan and met him.

"I just wanted to warn you that two of our friends are human."

Cain's eyes widened, and he turned toward Morven. "Hogan said something about humans living with you, but at the time, I was preoccupied and didn't ask about it. It's true, then?"

"It is. Orran, the dragon who was with me and the queen earlier, lives with one of them. Together, they tutor the prince. As for the other human, he lives with me." Morven touched his stomach, causing Cain to look down at it.

Hogan looked, too. He could only imagine what it felt like to be pregnant and carrying an egg. It was kind of terrifying and something he never wanted to live through. Morven seemed happy, though.

"So your baby . . ." Cain began, but he sounded like he wasn't sure how to continue.

"Will be a dragon and human hybrid, yes," Morven confirmed. "We're not sure what it will mean for them yet, but I suppose we'll find out soon enough."

"You don't have much longer before laying the egg, do you?"

"No. I'm excited, and even more so now that apparently, my baby will have two friends right from the start."

Cain smiled, which made Hogan smile, too. This was perfect. Cain's baby would be able to play with Blue as well as Morven and Sheldon's baby, which made Hogan feel like this was destiny. The three of them would be too close in age for it not to be.

He'd done the right thing. He'd known all along, but he'd expected Morven and the queen to disagree with him. Instead, they were giving Cain a home and a safe place to raise his baby.

Hogan would make sure of that.

Cain was wary as they reached another two massive doors. These were open, and he could hear people on the other side of it. It was mostly the sound of plates and growls, and he understood why when he stepped in.

The room was full of dragons. It was a familiar sight. Back with the Eiloren clan, Cain had been part of the team that cleaned up after the meals. It meant he hadn't been allowed to eat with the other dragons, but instead, he'd had to watch from the sidelines and wait until they finished. He looked around, looking for the team that would do the same, but he couldn't see anyone. Maybe they were hidden in another room. It didn't matter because his attention moved on to a small group sitting at a table under a window.

When Morven had confirmed that two humans lived here, Cain hadn't been sure what to expect. There weren't any humans in the Eiloren clan, and while the dragons there spent part of their time in their human form, it wasn't the same. He could see the humans now, though, and he was fascinated, especially to see that two dragons were sitting with them. They were in their human forms, and the four of them were talking.

Cain swallowed. He had no idea what was about to happen, but Morven and Hogan both guided him toward that small group, so he went. He owed them a lot, and he wasn't going to kick up a fuss when he didn't need to. Still, he clutched his egg closer to his chest, just in case. It wasn't that he didn't trust the humans or the dragons sitting with them, but rather that he didn't trust *anyone* right now. Any of the dragons in the room could try to take his egg, and he wouldn't allow that to happen.

"Relax," Hogan murmured. "I promised to keep you safe, and I meant it. Besides, those four won't hurt you. If anything, they'll protect you."

Cain was startled. "But two of them are human."

"It doesn't mean they're weak. Trust me. They're not, and they showed it. Blake, for example, helped Orran bring back the prince when his egg was taken by humans. He and Orran spent days running away from humans in the forest, and Blake protected Orran when he was wounded. It's when they fell in love, and Blake was the first human to move in with us."

"What about the other one?"

"Sheldon is Blake's brother. He went looking for him and was kidnapped. We rescued him, and while things haven't been easy for either of them, they're stronger than they look."

By the time Hogan was done explaining, they'd reached the table. The red dragon was the first to notice them, and they turned around, smiling. Their gaze stopped on Cain, and their eyes widened. "Hogan?" they asked.

Hogan glared. "Why do you always assume I did something?"

"Because usually, you do. *What* did you do this time?"

Cain was amused. Hogan had relaxed once they'd reached the small group, which told Cain they were his friends, maybe even people he considered family. It was good to know, because since Cain trusted Hogan and Hogan trusted them, Cain felt he could, too.

"Oh, he just went into the forest, found a pregnant runaway dragon, and helped him lay his egg," Morven said as he slid into a seat. He had to lean back because of how big his stomach was, something Cain understood well. "Then, instead of coming to me, he snuck said dragon into the palace and into his rooms," Morven continued.

By now, the attention of everyone at the table was on Cain. It flustered him, and he was grateful when Hogan put a hand on his shoulder and guided him toward one of the seats. He sat down, still holding his egg, but he forced himself to look up.

Everyone was still staring at him.

Morven cleared his throat. "This is Cain. He left the Eiloren clan because they wanted to take away his baby. He'll be staying with us. The queen has already talked to him, and while he's not a clan member yet, he probably will become one if he wants to eventually."

Cain smiled, and it wasn't forced. He'd known that was what the queen was saying, but he hadn't allowed himself to believe it would be this easy.

Not that it had been. He'd been terrified since he'd realized he was pregnant. When it had become noticeable, he'd been called into the office of the dragon in charge of those who took care of the eggs and babies. She'd ordered Cain to hand over his egg as soon as he laid it, and he'd had to agree, even though it was a lie. He'd needed to say yes to give him time to plan his escape. He should have left sooner, but he hadn't had the opportunity, especially after talking to the baby's other father.

All of that was over, though. Cain and his egg were safe, and they were never going back.

"I'll grab you a plate," Hogan said.

He looked around the table before leaving, and Cain was pretty sure he was mentally threatening everyone to be nice to him. He still didn't know what to think of Hogan's protective streak, but he was grateful for it.

Still, as soon as Hogan had left, everyone was on him.

"I'm Octavia," the red dragon said. "Female, as the name says."

"Cain, and I'm a male," Cain said.

Octavia nodded and pointed around the table. "That's Slavin, male. Then you have Sheldon, obviously male and human, and Blake, same. You already know Morven."

Cain's head spun, but he smiled at everyone.

"So Hogan helped you lay your egg," Sheldon said.

His gaze was fixed on the egg Cain was still holding, which made Cain bristle, even though he could understand why. Sheldon was the father of Morven's child, and from what Morven had said, they had no idea how their baby would turn out or what would happen to it. As far as Cain could remember, he'd never met a dragon and human hybrid, and he hoped everything would be okay. These people were good, and they deserved happiness. Besides, it had to be strange for a human to see an egg.

Even for dragons, it didn't happen often. There weren't a lot of dragons around. While most of them were fertile, it only happened once every few years, and when it did, it didn't mean the dragon wanted to be pregnant. Plus not everyone who wanted to managed to conceive. That meant few babies were born, and all of them were precious. It was one of the reasons Cain's old clan took all the eggs from the parents. They didn't want to waste their potential, or something like that.

But Cain wouldn't have to give up his baby. That was enough for him to want to stay with the Ogorth clan, and he hoped he would be allowed to. He realized it wouldn't be easy, though. The queen had said there had been problems, and Cain suspected it had to do with the humans. His king wouldn't have hesitated to kill them, but here, they'd found a place and a home. Some dragons were bound not to be happy about that. They also wouldn't be happy about welcoming a new dragon, although that might be slightly easier.

Cain hoped so.

"Are you done interrogating him?" Hogan asked. His voice was stern, but when Cain turned around, he noticed that Hogan's lips were twitching into a tiny smile. He was holding two plates, and he put one of them down in front of Cain.

"We're just curious," Blake said. "It's not every day you're so nice to someone. Did you hit your head?"

Hogan growled and settled into the seat next to Cain. "Shut your mouth. I didn't hit anything."

"Maybe not, but apparently, you help lay eggs," Octavia teased.

Cain relaxed in his seat. He'd never had this, and he wasn't sure he did now. These people weren't his friends yet. He could see himself settling down with them, though. He could see himself becoming friends with them and them teasing him in the future.

For now, though, he focused on his food and his egg. He didn't know what the future would be like, but he felt safe for the first time in forever and like there was a chance for him to be happy. He wasn't going to waste that worrying when there was nothing he could do.

Chapter Three

Cain was lost. He didn't like to admit it, not even to himself, but he was, and he was starting to panic.

Hogan had pushed him to go out on a flight, but Cain had been hesitant. He hadn't wanted to leave the egg alone, which was why Hogan had offered to stay in and keep an eye on it. Cain realized it was stupid. No one would try to touch his egg, especially not when it was in Hogan's rooms. Still, he'd been happy Hogan had offered, and he'd agreed. He hadn't even thought about the fact that he didn't know the palace and that he would probably have trouble finding Hogan's rooms again.

He looked around. The hallway looked the same on both the left and the right, and he had no idea which way to go. He remembered what floor Hogan's rooms were on, so he was sure that eventually, he could find them, but the palace was huge, so much bigger than anything he was used to.

Then there was the fact that people were walking around. Most of them were in their dragon form, although a few were in their human form. All of them had eyed Cain as if they wanted to talk to him, and he suspected that the only reason they hadn't was Hogan. As far as Cain knew, Hogan hadn't hurt anyone, but he knew Hogan's reputation, and he wouldn't be surprised if a dragon or two ended up with a black eye for looking at him too long. He didn't know why Hogan was so protective of him, and now wasn't the best moment to analyze his feelings, even though he felt funny inside every time he thought about it.

He looked to his left again, then to his right. His knees almost buckled at the sight of Orran coming toward him down the hallway. He was in his human form, so Cain quickly shifted.

"Good morning," Orran said when he reached Cain.

Cain found himself smiling. It was hard not to now that he was getting to know Orran. The other dragon had been intimidating at first, especially since he was so close to the queen, but he was a sweetheart, and Cain was glad to be able to relax. "Good morning."

Orran looked around Cain. "I have to say I'm surprised to see you on your own. Isn't Hogan your shadow by now?"

Cain's cheeks heated. "Not exactly. He told me to go out and fly since it had been too long in his opinion, but I didn't want to leave the egg alone."

Orran's eyebrows rose. "So he stayed with your egg?"

"Yes."

"You trust him that much?"

Cain shrugged. "Why not? He was the one who helped me in the forest. He brought me here and stood up for me so I wouldn't be kicked out. He hasn't done anything to suggest that I shouldn't trust him." It was still hard. Cain didn't want to trust anyone with his egg, and he was terrified someone would take it away from him. But like he'd just explained, Hogan hadn't done anything to show him he shouldn't be trusted, and Cain wanted and needed to go along with that.

"That's good to hear," Orran said with a smile. "Are you headed back?"

Cain rubbed the back of his neck. "I was trying to, but I got lost."

Orran chuckled. "It happens even to those of us who have lived here all their lives. I can show you where Hogan's rooms are, but maybe you'd like to come with me?"

"Where are you going?"

"To Blue."

Cain knew Blue was the queen's only child, and Cain was stunned by Orran's offer. No one had been able to go anywhere close to the Eiloren's king children. "Wouldn't your queen be against that?"

"She wants Blue to meet as many people as possible, especially when it comes to outsiders. I haven't asked about you specifically, but it's not like I'd leave you alone with the prince. I can talk to her, if you feel more comfortable."

"I just don't want her to be angry at me."

"She won't be. She trusts Blake and me, and she knows we wouldn't do anything to hurt her son. I can just walk you back to Hogan's rooms, though."

Both offers were tempting. This was the first time Cain was away from his egg since he'd laid it, and he felt the need to go back. On the other hand, he realized he probably needed some training when it came to baby dragons. He'd never been involved with young dragons, and he wasn't sure where to start. He would have to learn when his child came out of their egg, and today seemed like a good day to start. He wouldn't be alone with Blue, and hopefully, Orran and Blake would show him what to do.

"I'll come with you," he agreed.

Orran smiled and guided him down the hallway. Cain had many questions, but he didn't want to overwhelm or offend Orran. "Are you always in your human form when you spend time with the prince?" he asked after a few moments.

"Not always, no. But Blake is with me most of the time I spend with the prince, and it makes sense for me to be in my human form."

"I know that for your clan, it's not usual."

"Not for the oldest of us. I suppose we were trying to distance ourselves from the humans after what they did to our kind. The youngest dragons don't have that past with humanity, and they don't have prejudices when it comes to shifting. It's changing, though."

"Thanks to Blake and Sheldon."

"Exactly. I had no idea what to think when I first met Blake, but I'm glad I did."

Cain understood that. He was glad he'd met Hogan, although he doubted that he and Hogan would end up together the way Orran and Blake had. Still, they were a great couple to look up to, and Cain hoped that eventually he would have what they had. First, though, he had to focus on his egg and becoming part of this clan. When he'd escaped the Eiloren clan, he'd thought he would spend the rest of his life alone with his baby. He hadn't thought it possible that anyone would welcome them with open arms, but that was what the Ogorth clan had done. Some dragons weren't happy with Cain's presence, but so far, they'd stayed away from him. Hopefully, that would continue until their displeasure faded and Cain truly became part of the clan.

Orran stopped in front of a door. It looked normal, unlike the throne room doors, and Cain was surprised for a moment. It made sense not to want to advertise where the prince was, though.

Orran pushed open the door and stepped in. There was a loud screech, and something hit Orran right in the chest. He stumbled back, causing Cain to have to put his hands on Orran's hips to hold him up. He snatched them away as soon as Orran was steady, but Orran didn't seem to have noticed. He was focused on what had hit him.

It was a baby dragon. The prince was staring at Cain with wide eyes and a mouthful of teeth. Cain was pretty sure that was a smile, but not a hundred percent, so he stayed away.

"What have I already told you about throwing yourself on people that way?" Orran asked.

Blue didn't answer. He didn't even look at Orran. He was

still staring at Cain, and Cain shuffled his feet, unsure what to do or say. Should he bow? Blue was still a baby, so he wouldn't care, but it would be proper.

Before he had time to decide, Orran set Blue on the floor. The baby stayed where he was, but that gave Cain the opportunity to look around. The room they were in looked like a sitting room, full of couches made for dragons and a few chairs for humans. The windows were wide and the curtains were open, allowing sunlight to stream in. The coffee table placed between the couches was covered with plates full of sandwiches and drinks. Blake was sitting in one of the chairs, looking at Orran and Blue and smiling. Cain felt out of place, but it wasn't like he could turn around and leave, so he waited until Blake turned his attention to him and smiled at him.

"I didn't expect Orran to bring anyone," Blake said, getting to his feet.

"It was a spur-of-the-moment decision," Orran said. He moved toward Blake, kissing the top of his head and smiling down at him. The sight made Cain's chest tighten. It was so obvious they were happy and in love, and he wanted the same.

"Well, whatever happened, I'm happy to see you. I'm exhausted. He's wanted to play the entire morning, so it's your turn now."

"I could do it," Cain offered.

Both Blake and Orran stared at him. "What?" Blake asked.

"Why not? I'm going to have a baby soon. I can probably use the training."

Blake gestured at the floor. "Feel free. Do you want to eat something first?"

Cain shook his head, then sat on the floor, hoping he wasn't making a mistake. He allowed the prince to come closer at his own pace. He was fascinated by the sight of the baby, and his hands itched to touch him. He couldn't wait until his own baby hatched and he was able to raise them.

It didn't take long for the prince to realize he could trust Cain. Cain was surprised, but maybe he shouldn't have been. The Ogorth clan did things differently than Cain's old clan, and babies clearly knew they could trust the people around them. Before half an hour had passed, Blue was climbing all over him, and Cain was laughing.

This was much better than being alone in the forest. He didn't know what would happen next, but as long as he could stay with the Ogorth clan, he knew he'd be happy.

Hogan had taken the egg to work with him. When Cain had been hesitant about going to fly, he'd known he had to do something. Cain wouldn't go without his egg, and while he could use the harness Morven had found for them, Hogan had wanted Cain to go on his own. It was hard for him, but he had to understand that he could trust the clan with his baby, especially Hogan. That was why Hogan had sent him out without telling him he had to go to work. Hopefully, Cain would still trust him when he didn't find him in the room they still shared. Just in case, though, he'd left a note.

It was odd to have the harness on his chest. The egg was bigger and heavier than Hogan remembered. It was a steady presence against his chest, a presence that made him smile every time he moved, and he couldn't avoid noticing it.

It didn't make him rethink his thoughts about having children, but he supposed that as long as others laid eggs, he would be happy to babysit.

Octavia kept eyeing Hogan as if she expected something to happen, which made Hogan want to ask her what was going on. He knew what it was, though, so he kept his mouth shut until she couldn't take it anymore.

It's strange to see you with a baby, she commented.

It's not a baby. For now, it's an egg.

Octavia rolled her eyes. *You know what I mean.*

Hogan did. He looked down at the egg, but in his dragon form, he couldn't see it well. He wanted to check up on it, so he shifted to his human form. The harness was much too big for this form, but he still kept it on his shoulders, holding the egg with his hands and looking down at it.

It was a pale yellow, but he could see traces of a darker color when he looked closer. It was impossible to tell what color it was, but it was enough to tell him that the egg's other father wasn't a yellow dragon like Cain. It was almost as if Hogan himself was the other father, and the thought flustered him so much that he had to focus on something else. The problem was that Octavia wasn't on board with that.

She shifted, too, and moved closer to the egg. Hogan found himself holding it steadily and slowly turning away from them, something that made her eyebrows shoot high on her forehead. "You know I'm not going to hurt it, right?" she asked.

"I'm aware."

"Why are you protecting it from me, then?"

Hogan didn't have an answer to that, not a real one anyway. "Cain trusted me with his child. If he doesn't tell me you're allowed to touch the egg, I'm sorry, but I can't let you do it."

Octavia stared at him for a moment, then nodded. "I understand. You know, I didn't think you'd be good at this, but you're great. Cain is lucky to have you."

Hogan wasn't too sure about that, but before he could protest, someone else in the security room snorted softly.

Hogan frowned and looked around, searching for the person who had made the noise. It might have nothing to do with the conversation he was having with Octavia, but until he was sure, he would be tense.

His gaze landed on a dark green dragon. His color was

murky, unlike Morven's, which made Hogan dislike him from the start. The dragon was staring at him and the egg, and Hogan bristled. "You have a problem?" he asked.

The dragon glared, then shifted. Hogan was surprised, because usually people tended not to want to have conversations with him.

"First humans, now this," the dragon spat out. "Our clan is going to lose all credibility with other clans."

Hogan blinked. "What are you talking about? You think we'll lose credibility because we offer a safe haven for parents and their children?"

"He should go back to his own clan. He's not part of ours, and he doesn't belong here."

Hogan was getting pissed. Apparently Octavia noticed, because she reached for his arm and squeezed. Hogan was ready to step back because he had to take care of the egg, but unfortunately, the green dragon wasn't done.

"If I knew what clan he came from, I would contact them myself. We don't have infinite resources. We can't afford to continue taking in people who don't belong here. I suppose it's better than humans, though. At least he's a dragon."

Hogan was still holding the egg, but he handed it to Octavia. She blinked and looked like she didn't want to take it, but he glared at her until she did. He knew she would keep it safe.

He untied the harness from his body, dropping it on the floor, then stepped toward the green dragon.

The male seemed to realize he'd made a mistake, and his eyes widened as he took a step back and raised his hands. "What are you doing?" he asked.

"What were you saying about Cain? Oh, and please repeat what you are saying about Blake and Sheldon, too. I'm sure Morven and the queen will enjoy hearing what you have to say about their choices."

"You know I'm right. Those three don't belong here.

They're not part of the clan, and I'm not the only one who thinks that way."

Hogan was done listening to him. Whatever he had to say, it wasn't important, but it was offending. Hogan raised his arm and punched the green dragon in the eye.

The green dragon yowled and stumbled back, hitting the wall. He covered his face with his hand, making Hogan snort.

"I didn't hit you that hard," he said. But he was going to.

He stepped closer, ready to do just that, but Octavia grabbed his arm again. Hogan glared at her, but she shook her head. "Stop that. Morven is going to be pissed when he finds out what you just did."

"I'm pretty sure he's going to wish he'd been here so he could hit that asshole himself."

"Maybe so, but Cain trusted you with his egg. You need to stay with it and keep an eye on it, not hand it over to me."

"I trust you, and I'm sure he does, too."

"It doesn't matter." She held out the egg. "Take it and go back to Cain. I think you should take the rest of the day off."

That sounded like a good idea, since Hogan still felt the need to hit everyone in the room. Thankfully, only the green dragon had said anything, but everyone was looking at him cautiously as if they expected him to start beating up all of them.

Hogan huffed and took the egg. He cradled it to his chest, smiling at the weight of it. He was already getting used to carrying it around, something he hadn't expected.

"That smile makes you even creepier," Octavia said. "You're scaring everyone."

Hogan widened the smile, making sure his teeth were showing. "Then my job here is done. I *want* everyone to be afraid of me, so much that they won't even think about badmouthing Blake, Sheldon, or Cain."

Octavia patted Hogan's shoulder. "I'm pretty sure you

managed. Now go to Cain. Bring his egg back to him, but please, calm down before you reach him. You don't want him to freak out at the thought of what just happened. The last thing he needs is to be scared of you."

Hogan didn't like that thought. He didn't want Cain to be afraid of anything, but especially not of him. "I'll make sure he isn't."

Octavia nodded. "Good." She hesitated. "It's good to see you care about someone that much."

"What are you talking about?"

"You know. You've always been on your own, and while I know you love our friends, you're still distant. You care about Cain, though."

Hogan wanted to protest and say that wasn't the case, but he couldn't, because she was right. He didn't know when it had happened or why, but somewhere along the way, Cain had become important to him. He was so important that Hogan wanted to do everything he could to make Cain happy and safe, which wasn't something he usually felt with people he barely knew.

He did with Cain, though.

When Cain got back to the rooms he still shared with Hogan, they were empty. He had a moment of panic when he couldn't find the egg, but he breathed in and out and told himself that he trusted Hogan to keep his baby safe, which meant he shouldn't be afraid. Hogan was probably off visiting his friends, or maybe he'd gone to work. He hadn't said anything about it, so Cain wasn't sure, but he was certain Hogan would make sure nothing happened to the egg.

Still, when the door opened about ten minutes later, he jumped to his feet and rushed toward it. Hogan walked in, holding Cain's egg, with the harness hanging from his shoulder. He jerked back when Cain reached him, but only for a second. Cain realized it was because he hadn't recognized him.

"I didn't expect you to be back so soon," Hogan said. "Did you find my note?"

Cam shook his head. "What note? I just came back, so I didn't have the time to look around."

"I left it in the nest. I knew you'd be looking for the egg."

Cain turned around, and sure enough, he noticed a piece of paper in the nest he hadn't seen earlier. He walked back to get it. *Had to go to work. Your baby is safe with me.*

Cain snorted and looked at Hogan. "You think I wouldn't have freaked out?"

"I don't know, but I'd hoped you wouldn't. You had no reason to."

"Shouldn't you be at work, then?"

"Octavia told me to go home early."

Hogan wasn't saying everything, but Cain knew better than to ask. He wasn't even sure he wanted to know what was happening. Since he'd moved in with the clan, he'd noticed that Hogan was protective of him, and he wouldn't be surprised if he'd hit someone because they said something they shouldn't have. From what Octavia and the others had told him, it was something Hogan did fairly often. He had very few people he cared about in his life, but he protected all of them, even from words. Cain was grateful, but it also confused him.

Cain shuffled his feet. "Well, I should probably go." If he didn't, he would start hoping that what Hogan was doing meant something more than it did.

Hogan frowned and took a step back, taking the egg with him. Cain wasn't afraid, though. He trusted Hogan, and he knew Hogan wouldn't do anything to hurt the baby. "What are you talking about? You just came back," Hogan asked.

And he'd come back late. He'd played with Blue for almost half an hour, and it had been a delight. It made Cain look forward to the day when his egg hatched, and he couldn't wait. He wouldn't have hurried back if he'd known Hogan and the egg wouldn't even be here.

"I was talking about the rooms the queen offered," he said quietly. When she had, he'd been tempted to say yes right away, but he'd felt safer with Hogan. Now that he'd been staying with Hogan for a while, he didn't want to leave anymore.

These were Hogan's rooms, though, and he no doubt wanted his privacy back. Besides, Cain was safe now. He didn't need Hogan to protect him.

"You want to move out?" Hogan asked.

His voice was flat, and it made Cain wonder what was going through his mind. It was always hard to tell.

"Well, you were kind to offer your rooms for me and my egg to stay, but we don't have to anymore. I'm sure you're looking forward to getting your privacy and freedom back."

Hogan shook his head. "You don't have to go." He paused and frowned. When he continued, he sounded hesitant. "I like having you around."

Cain was stunned. "You do?"

"It's nice not to be alone."

Cain stared. Hogan had never said anything about feeling lonely, but then Cain supposed he hadn't been since Cain had entered his life. Hogan had friends, though. Why did he feel that way? Cain supposed he could understand when it came to Hogan's rooms. He lived alone, and while Cain had assumed he liked it that way, maybe he'd been wrong. "You're lonely?"

Hogan shrugged. He walked to the nest, gently putting the egg down and wrapping it in blankets. "I grew up with three parents, then lived with other recruits and guards when I started training to enter palace security. I only got these rooms when Orran became Blue's tutor and Morven was promoted to his job. He gave a promotion to the entire team, and it came with private rooms. It seemed like a good idea to accept, but I realized it didn't feel right after only a few days."

Cain looked around. The rooms weren't luxurious, but they were cozy, and he liked being here. It was better than having to live on his own, so he understood where Hogan was coming from. Maybe it was because he had also never been on his own. When he'd been a child, he'd lived with the other young dragons of the clan. Once it had been decided he would be part of the cleaning teams, he'd been moved to the dormitories, which, again, he'd had to share. Sharing with Hogan was nothing like that, and Cain quite liked it.

"But you can go if you'd rather," Hogan continued. He sounded flustered now, and he wasn't looking at Cain, which wasn't like him.

"I said that only because I thought you'd want your rooms back," Cain murmured. "I'm grateful you offered me a place to stay, but you don't have to anymore. I don't want to impose."

"You're not. I just told you I want you to stay, but I won't force you. I can help you move, if you need me to."

It sounded as if Hogan already regretted offering for Cain to stay with him, but Cain knew better. Even though he and Hogan didn't know each other well, he'd already started to learn the other dragon. Hogan was flustered because he didn't usually show people that he could be vulnerable, including his friends. He wasn't trying to change Cain's mind or to tell him he didn't want him anymore. He was putting up his shields in case Cain wanted to leave.

Cain found himself smiling. "Since you so kindly offered, I'd like to stay here with you."

Hogan's shoulders relaxed, which told Cain he was right.

Hogan had expected him to refuse and leave, but until Hogan asked him to, he wasn't going anywhere.

"Good," Hogan said. He cleared his throat. "It's almost lunchtime. Do you want to go to the dining room?"

Cain blinked. He hadn't expected the quick change of topic, although maybe he should have. This was what Hogan did. Now that he had his answers, he was pushing the vulnerability away and acting as if it didn't exist.

"We can go," he said. He enjoyed spending time with Hogan, but also with their small group of friends. He would never have thought it possible, but he had friends now. They were mostly Hogan's, but they'd welcomed Cain, and he knew that in time, they could become like family. It was all he wanted.

He'd never had a family. He'd never known his parents or even who they were, and he didn't want his child to go through that. They deserved better, and so did Cain. He wouldn't have any of this if he'd stayed with the Eiloren clan, but he hadn't. He'd been brave enough for his child and for himself. He'd run away and had freed both of them from the expectations and the life waiting for them. Now, he had a new future. He didn't know what it held for him apart from the fact that he and his child would be safe, and hopefully, happy.

That was all he could ask for, even though he wanted so much more. He wanted a relationship, someone to love and who would love him.

And for whatever reason, when he thought about that, the only dragon he could see by his side was Hogan.

Hogan kept peeking at Cain as they walked to the dining room. Cain had strapped the egg to his chest, but he was still holding the bottom of it with both his hands as he walked.

He'd wanted to move out. Hogan couldn't believe it, yet at

the same time, he could. Of course Cain wanted to move out. The only reason he was living with Hogan right now was that Hogan had brought him to his rooms when they'd first met. The queen had offered Cain his own set of rooms, but Hogan hadn't even thought about the possibility that Cain would agree. Even though Cain had been staying with him only for a few days, he was used to his presence, and he didn't want to lose it.

He didn't want to lose Cain.

He realized it was stupid. Cain wasn't his to lose, and even if he moved out, it wasn't like he was leaving the mountain. He would always be there if Hogan wanted to talk to him, but it wouldn't be the same, and Hogan disliked thinking about what his life would be like if Cain wasn't in it constantly the way he was now.

So Hogan had exposed his feelings. He wasn't used to it. His parents and friends knew how he was, and they could read him better than he could understand himself some days. But Cain was new, and he couldn't do the same. That was the only reason Hogan had told him how he felt, and he was grateful Cain hadn't used those feelings against him. There was still time, he supposed, but he trusted Cain not to.

He didn't know *why* he did, but apparently, being there when someone laid their egg brought you closer to that person. It had for Hogan anyway, but then he supposed he wasn't going to help lay any more eggs anytime soon. It wasn't his job, and he didn't want to do it. He was grateful he'd been there for Cain, but it had been terrifying and not something Hogan was looking forward to repeating.

None of that explained why he was so fascinated by Cain and why he didn't want him to leave, but Hogan had never been one to analyze his feelings. He felt the way he felt, and that was that.

But he realized that eventually, Cain would either leave or

want more from him, and he didn't know which was worse. He didn't wish for Cain to go, but he also didn't want to make himself vulnerable. That was why he didn't have relationships. He couldn't trust people he didn't already know, which meant that if he wanted a relationship, it had to be with someone he already trusted, like his friends.

The thought of being with Octavia or Slavin made him shudder in horror. They were friends and nothing more. Hogan had never wanted anything more with them.

Cain was different. He wasn't Hogan's friend yet, but Hogan trusted him, and he was pretty sure that even though Cain wasn't his friend, he was something different and more precious.

"Have you listened to anything I told you?" Cain suddenly asked.

Hogan blinked at him. "You were talking about . . . the palace?"

Thankfully, Cain didn't seem offended. "I suppose I started with that, but I left that topic behind a while ago. I was telling you that I met Blue this morning."

"How?" Even though Hogan was someone both the queen and Morven trusted with their lives, he'd barely spent any time with the prince. How had Cain managed to get to him?

"I met Orran in the hallway. I was lost, and he offered to take me back to your rooms. He also asked if I wanted to meet Blue, and I said yes. I guess I wanted to see a baby dragon. It was the first time, and I even got to play with him."

Hogan shook his head. "I don't understand the way your old clan does things. Why do they isolate baby dragons? It doesn't make sense."

Cain sighed. "I don't know. I think it's about control. But I'm scared about not being able to take care of my baby when they come out of the egg, and spending time with Blue helped relieve me. I'm still afraid, but I know I can do it."

"And you won't be doing it alone. That has to count for something."

Cain's smile was blinding. "It does. When I escaped, I thought I would be doing this on my own in the forest. It was kind of terrifying, but I would have been free. Now, I *am* free, but I'm not alone, and I couldn't imagine doing this on my own anymore, not after meeting you."

The thought of taking care of a baby sent Hogan in a panic, but he managed not to show it. If Cain needed him to be a second parent, he would do it, even though he'd never imagined himself in that role.

Thankfully, they'd reached the dining room, and Hogan didn't have to answer.

The doors were open, and they walked in. Hogan immediately looked toward the corner where he and his friends usually sat, and sure enough, Sheldon and Blake were already there. They were talking and seemingly not noticing that some of the dragons in the room were glaring at them, but Hogan suspected they'd seen it. They knew who wasn't happy to have them there, and after what had happened to them when Sheldon had moved into the palace, they knew to be careful.

Hogan didn't like that. This was Sheldon and Blake's home, and they shouldn't have to be careful when they walked around. As he and Cain passed one of the glaring dragons, Hogan growled and snapped his teeth. They jumped, looking guilty. Hogan was pleased when they decided they would have lunch away from the dining room and scuttled out.

"You're very protective of your friends," Cain said.

"They're my family."

Cain nodded. "That's what I thought. They're lucky to have you."

Hogan wanted to tell Cain that he had him, too, but he

didn't. The words felt too fragile, and so did he. Instead, he guided Cain toward the table and watched him slide into one of the empty seats. It had become their habit by now that Hogan was the one who went to grab plates, so he left Cain with Sheldon and Blake to do just that.

When he came back with the food, the three of them were talking. "I promise, things are going better," Sheldon was saying. "It was a bit touch-and-go for a while when I first arrived, especially after Blake and I were attacked, but it's okay."

Cain's eyes were wide. "You were attacked?"

"Not everyone was happy to have humans here. Some are still grumbling about it, but they stopped trying to talk to us and tell us to go back to where we came from. I take that as a win, and I think you should, too."

"It's just so different. Back with my old clan, people barely even looked at me. It's uncomfortable when so many people are staring, you know?"

Hogan sat next to Cain and pushed his plate toward him. "Who's staring?" he asked.

Cain waved at the room in general. "Take your pick. I feel like I'm always on display."

Hogan looked around. Sure enough, dragons were still staring. One of them was at the table right next to theirs, and Hogan growled at them.

"Stop growling at people," Blake said, sounding amused.

Hogan crossed his arms over his chest and glared. "I'll stop when they stop staring and saying bad things."

"That's why you growled?" Cain asked in a whisper. He sounded like he didn't quite believe it.

"Why else? I don't want anyone to make you uneasy. This is your home now, and they should get used to it." He paused. "The same goes for Sheldon and Blake."

"Aww, I didn't know you cared so much," Blake said.

"You're my friends." Hogan wasn't sure when they'd

become friends instead of just being Orran and Morven's men, but it didn't matter. They were, and he always protected his friends.

"Does that mean I'm your friend, too?" Cain asked.

Hogan wanted to tell him that he was so much more, but he was afraid, both of his own feelings and of Cain's possible reaction. Cain was going through too much. He didn't need to have to deal with Hogan's feelings, too. "You are," Hogan confirmed.

Cain looked a bit sad, and Hogan couldn't begin to imagine why that was. He was relieved when Cain smiled, and it was a real smile, one he usually reserved for his egg. "Good. Because you're my friend, too."

It wasn't nearly enough, but for now, it would have to be.

By the time lunch was on its way, Hogan was pissed. He wanted to keep an eye on the asshole who'd been staring, but it wasn't easy, since they were so many of them. Since that one was the closest, Hogan made sure he knew he was being watched. He was smug when the dragon finally got up to leave, but he only had a few moments to focus on his food before Morven, who had arrived earlier, leaned closer to him. "You wanted to kick his ass, didn't you?" he asked in a whisper.

Hogan glared at his plate. "Didn't you?"

There was a pause before Morven answered. "I did. I dislike that all the dragons keep staring at Sheldon and Blake, and now, Cain. It might not be a bad thing, though."

"If it makes Cain uncomfortable, it is."

"I agree, but some of them might only be curious. Not everyone wants to kick them out, you know?"

"I wouldn't be so sure. I've heard whispers, and a dragon confronted me earlier. They're not happy that the queen has allowed humans to stay with us, and Cain is the last straw.

The dragon who confronted me said that if they knew which clan Cain came from, they would contact them and hand him over." The thought made Hogan want to look for that dragon and stab him with his fork, and he peeked around, wondering if they were having lunch.

Morven put a hand on Hogan's wrist. "Hogan, you're not just a guard anymore. You can't go around kicking people's asses just because you don't like what they're saying."

"I was thinking about using my fork this time."

Morven half-snorted, half-laughed. He let go of Hogan's wrist and patted his lips with his napkin before answering. "I'm pretty sure stabbing them would be even worse. I understand where you're coming from. Some days I want to snap at them, too. But just like I'm not only a guard anymore, you're not, either."

"You could have fooled me when you sent me to patrol the forest." But Morven was right. Hogan still was a palace guard, but he now belonged to a smaller team, a team in charge of the other guards. That was why he and Octavia had been in the security room earlier. They were supposed to supervise the people who kept an eye on the cameras and make sure everything was working all right and nothing was wrong. Hogan had made sure they knew he was disappointed by the fact that they hadn't noticed Cain entering the forest.

Watching them squirm had been fun.

Morven huffed. "Are you still holding that against me? I already explained why I did it, and besides, you wouldn't have met Cain if I hadn't sent you out. Try not to beat anyone up, and I won't send you on forest patrol anymore."

Hogan wouldn't win this. He could try arguing with Morven, but unless he wanted a demotion, this was what his life would be like from now on. He'd never wanted to be in charge, but now that Cain and the egg were in his life, he was grateful for the private rooms. He didn't want to lose them and have Cain move out, which meant he had to stop beating people up.

No one had said anything about growling at them, though.

"And don't think I don't know you punched someone earlier," Morven said, turning back to his plate. "Was it the guy who said he wanted to find Cain's clan?"

Hogan had to make a conscious effort to loosen his hold on his fork. "It was, and I don't regret it. Don't ask me to apologize to that dragon, because I'd rather go on forest patrol."

The corner of Morven's lips curled. "I won't ask you that. If I had it my way, I would punch his other eye. But remember that you can't continue doing that."

"I'll try," Hogan grumbled.

He might understand why Morven wanted him to stop beating up people, but if it meant protecting Cain and their friends, he would continue glaring and growling. Hopefully that would be enough to keep the offending dragons in line at the very least.

Cain was chatting with Sheldon and Blake on the other side of the table, and since he was distracted, he didn't see the dragons looking his way. Hogan did, though, and he spent the rest of the meal snarling and snapping his teeth as quietly as he could. Morven looked amused more than angry, so Hogan took that as a win and continued.

He wanted to protect Cain and keep him happy. He didn't know why or even if he would be able to do that, but he was certainly going to try. That was why when Cain said he enjoyed the cake that had been put out for dessert, he jumped to his feet and went to grab a second slice. On his way back, he snapped his teeth at a dragon who was headed toward their table. The dragon scrambled back to their seat.

He put the plate in front of Cain, earning himself a beaming smile.

"You didn't have to," Cain said.

Hogan shrugged. "You said you enjoyed it, and I know you have a sweet tooth."

Cain's cheeks flushed. "You're right. I do."

Morven knocked his shoulder against Hogan's. Hogan sighed, thinking Morven was going to berate him for snapping his teeth at that dragon, but instead, Morven murmured, "Are you interested in him?"

For a second, Hogan thought he was talking about the dragon he'd snapped his teeth at. But no, of course. Morven was talking about Cain, just like Octavia had been earlier. "Why is everyone asking me that?"

Morven arched a brow. "Maybe because it's kind of obvious? I've never seen you act this way with someone. You're protective of him, more than of anyone else in our little group."

"Only because I feel responsible for him."

Morven continued staring, and since Hogan didn't have anything left to eat on his plate, he couldn't act as if he wasn't aware of it. He scowled at Morven, but Morven was used to it, and he wasn't intimidated. "Are you sure that's all?" he asked.

"What do you want me to say?" Hogan asked with a growl.

Morven shook his head and leaned back. He pressed both his hands on his stomach, and Hogan couldn't stop himself from looking down. Luckily, Morven wasn't offended. "Whatever way you feel about him, I hope you realize that he and his baby are a package deal. He's done too much to keep the baby safe, and he won't discard them, not even for you."

Hogan bristled. "I would never ask him to do that."

"I never said you would. If anything, I know you'll protect both of them with your life if you have to. But I also know that you're not a family man. You don't deal well with children, and that's what's going to happen if you and Cain get together. You'll be a father, whether you want it or not. I think that's something you should keep in mind before doing anything."

"I'm very much aware of that, so you don't have to tell me. I might go around beating people up, but it doesn't mean I'm an idiot."

"You're right. I shouldn't have talked to you that way, and I apologize. I'm just worried, both about that and about you."

Hogan huffed and turned his attention back to Cain. Morven was right, though. If Hogan and Cain continued the way they were, eventually, Hogan would find himself in the role of a father. Cain hadn't asked him to, and Hogan doubted he would, but he wouldn't be able to avoid it once the egg hatched.

Was that what he wanted? He'd never thought he'd have children, but he wasn't entirely opposed to them. While it was true that he'd stayed away from Blue, that was mostly because he was the prince, not because he was a baby. Things would be different with Cain's child.

Or at least Hogan hoped so. He didn't want to lose Cain, which was what would happen if Hogan didn't step up to take care of the baby. Right now, the thought of losing Cain was worse than having to be a father, but Hogan would have to think about it.

When the egg hatched, Hogan needed to have everything under control.

Chapter Four

Cain rubbed the top of the egg, wondering how it could get so dirty when it didn't even move by itself. If he wasn't mistaken, that was a spot of chocolate, which was probably his fault from the cake he'd had for lunch. He always had cake for lunch, and he enjoyed it. Back with the Eiloren clan, he and the other cleaners had only been allowed to eat leftovers. That meant cake was never part of their meal, and he was enjoying it now that he could have as much of it as he could.

He was also enjoying Hogan's attention.

He still wasn't sure what was going on with Hogan. Everyone was acting as if Hogan's behavior wasn't like him, but Cain had never known him differently. He always made sure Cain had enough to eat and got two plates of dessert instead of one. He kept Cain's glass filled to the brink. He often asked Cain if he was hungry or thirsty, and if Cain answered positively, he gave him food or water. He was taking care of Cain when Cain didn't even know he needed someone to, and it made Cain wonder if maybe there was more to their relationship than either of them had expected.

He wanted there to be. He'd been with the Ogorth clan for a few weeks now, and he felt like he was home. He didn't want to move out of Hogan's rooms like he'd suggested a few days ago. He was glad Hogan hadn't agreed, because he didn't know what he would have done if he had.

Cain couldn't stop himself from smiling. Something was happening between him and Hogan, and while it was slow going, he had hope.

He finished cleaning the egg, then started wrapping it in some of the blankets in the nest. That was something he and Hogan needed to talk about. Hogan had left his nest to Cain, while he'd taken to sleeping just in front of it in his dragon form. He'd said it was to make sure he could protect Cain if anyone came in, but no one had tried, and they didn't have a reason to. Cain was aware that Hogan was doing it because he wanted him to be comfortable, and sharing a nest with someone he barely knew wouldn't have been in the beginning.

Things were different now. Cain would be more than comfortable sharing a nest with Hogan. When he closed his eyes, he could see them curled around each other, with the egg pressed against Cain's stomach. He wanted that so much that it surprised him, although maybe it shouldn't have. Of course he wanted a family. He'd never had a chance to have one, but now, he had all the opportunities in the world. He could shape his life the way he wanted without having to obey orders.

Someone tried to open the door, making him jerk back. He tensed, placing himself in front of the egg, even though he knew it had to be Hogan. He relaxed when he heard the sound of a key in the lock, but when the dragon came in, it wasn't Hogan.

Cain wasn't sure how he knew it. This dragon was black, too, and he suspected they were related to Hogan. Hogan had told him he had three parents, so this had to be one of them. Which one, though, Cain didn't know. He supposed he was about to find out.

He stayed where he was, waiting for the dragon to notice him. When they did, they jerked back, but they didn't leave. Instead, they stared until Cain was flustered.

Hello, he said. *My name is Cain. I'm a friend of Hogan's.*

The dragon smiled, which was kind of terrifying in their

dragon form. *I've heard about you, although I wish I could say it was from my son. I'm Freya.*

One of Hogan's mothers. Cain relaxed even more. Hogan trusted few people in his life, and his parents were part of that group. *It's a pleasure to meet you. Hogan isn't here right now.*

I suspected as much, which is why I used my key. I was just going to drop something off.

Now that Cain looked closer, he saw that Freya was holding a plate. A big slice of pie was sitting on it, and his mouth watered at the sight. Right now, there was nothing he wanted more than to eat that slice of pie.

Freya chuckled. *It's for you, actually. Hogan hasn't told us about you, but we heard the gossip. You have a sweet tooth, don't you?*

Cain was pretty sure he was blushing, even though he was in his dragon form. *I do. I wasn't allowed many sweets when I was with my old clan. I guess I'm making up for all the cake and pie I couldn't eat then.*

Freya's expression twisted, but she didn't look angry. *That's good. I wasn't aware you lived with my son, though.* Her gaze drifted to the egg that was barely hidden behind Cain. *I did know about your egg. Congratulations.*

Thank you. And yes, right now, I'm staying with Hogan. I think he wants to make sure I'm safe.

This was awkward. He'd never met anyone's parents. He didn't know how to deal with that or what to say, and he hoped Freya wouldn't think he was an idiot. He certainly felt like one.

Thankfully, the door opened again, and this time, it *was* Hogan. He froze when he walked in on Cain and his mother, and since he was in his human form, his surprise showed in his expression.

Cain quickly shifted. "Your mother is here," he said.

Hogan narrowed his eyes. "I can see that."

He was grumpy. Something had probably happened at

work, and if Cain knew Hogan, it no doubt had to do with him or Morven, Blake, and Sheldon. Hogan took his protector role very seriously, even though it was self-assigned. Cain had the impression that Hogan spent most of his days growling at people and threatening to stab them with his fork if they so much as looked at one of the people he cared about.

Freya shifted, too. In her human form, she was a few inches shorter than Hogan. They shared the color, but her black was lighter, almost a dark gray. "I brought some pie for Cain. I didn't know he was living with you, but I didn't know where to find him."

Hogan shrugged. In front of his mother, he almost behaved like a child. "I need to keep him safe."

"That's what Cain said, yes." But Freya wasn't convinced. Cain didn't need to know her to be aware of that. It was in her expression.

She probably didn't know what to think of the situation. Cain didn't, either, and he was living it.

She put her hands on her hips. "Well, that doesn't matter. I'd like for the two of you and the egg to have dinner with me, your mother, and your father."

Hogan made a strangled sound. "That's not going to be possible."

"No? Would you like to explain why?"

Hogan opened and closed his mouth a few times. "Cain would be overwhelmed. He's new here."

"I've been here a few weeks," Cain pointed out. That earned him a scowl from Hogan.

"See," Freya said. "Cain wants to come. Don't you, Cain?"

Cain wasn't sure who he was most afraid of right now. Probably Freya, so he nodded. "Of course. It would be a pleasure to meet all of Hogan's parents."

Freya beamed. "We agree, then. We'll be expecting you for dinner on Saturday evening. Make sure not to be late.

Hogan's other mother doesn't appreciate tardiness."

She was gone in a whirlwind, leaving Cain to gape at the now-closed door. He had no idea what had happened, but he turned to Hogan to make sure he was okay. Maybe he shouldn't have accepted that dinner invitation without talking to Hogan first. He doubted that anything he could have said would have changed Freya's mind, but he should have tried.

Hogan rubbed his face. "I'm sorry," he said.

Cain frowned. "For what?"

"My mother. She can be overwhelming sometimes. Well, most of the time, actually. You don't have to go to that dinner if you don't want to."

"I do want to go."

Seeing Hogan with his mother had made Cain think about his egg. Would he act this way, too, when his baby was an adult? Would he be overbearing but loving and worried? It was hard to think of himself as a father, even though he had an egg. Things would change once it hatched, and he couldn't wait.

Hogan wanted to die. That would probably be overkill, since he'd only had to deal with his mother, but he hadn't expected it. He'd wanted to keep Cain away from his family for as long as possible, but he'd failed. Now Cain was going to meet his other two parents, and Hogan didn't know how he would react.

Hogan was lucky. He didn't have two parents, but three, and all of them loved him. Cain had never known his, and Hogan had been afraid that meeting Hogan's and talking to them would wound him. So far, it didn't look like it, but that might change. "Don't feel obligated," he said.

Cain shook his head. "I don't. If you don't want me to go,

I won't, but I would like to. Your mother seemed like a nice person, and I expect your father and your other mother are, too."

"They are. I'm not surprised they want to meet you." Especially since Hogan had been avoiding their phone calls and texts.

He should have known they would do something like this. His mother had said she didn't know that Cain was living with him, and maybe she truly hadn't, but Cain was the reason she'd come in. Normally, she wouldn't have if Hogan wasn't home. He would have to have a chat with her. Now that Cain and his egg were living with him, his parents couldn't barge in whenever they wanted. Cain deserved his privacy, and Hogan would make sure he had it.

Cain sat in the nest and grabbed his egg. He looked happy, which was a surprise, considering what had just happened. Hogan usually wanted to run away screaming when he had to deal with his parents, but Cain looked at peace.

So Cain would meet Hogan's parents. Hogan knew what his parents would expect and what they would hope for, and he found himself hoping for the same. He and Cain were working together well, very much like a couple, except that they didn't share a nest and hadn't even kissed yet. It might be in their future, though. Hogan could too easily imagine it, and it became harder to resist the urge to kiss Cain every day that passed. Hogan couldn't deny he was in love, at least not to himself.

He didn't know how to bring it up. If he hadn't cared about Cain, he would just have kissed him and tumbled him into the nest. But Cain deserved so much more, and Hogan didn't know how to give him that. It was easier to focus on their routine and familiarity.

"How was your day?" he asked instead of telling Cain he was dying to kiss him.

Cain smiled up at him. "It was fine. I missed you at lunch."

"I'm sorry I wasn't there. Slavin and I had something to deal with for work." But Hogan had made sure Octavia kept an eye on Cain and the dragons still grumbling about his presence with the clan. When she'd come back to work after lunch, she'd sworn that no one had done anything, and Hogan had taken that as an explanation for her lack of punching people.

"Will you be at dinner, though?"

"That's why I came by. Are you ready to go, or do you want to wait a bit longer?"

"I'm not really hungry, not for dinner." But Cain kept peeking at the pie.

Cain wanted it, so Hogan snatched it from the table and brought it to Cain along with a fork. Cain took the plate with a smile while Hogan settled down in the nest next to him. Cain didn't hesitate to hand over his egg, and the clear sign of trust touched Hogan. He gently cradled the egg to his chest, stroking the delicate surface.

Cain was focused on his pie, so Hogan turned his attention to the egg. It was clean and gleaming in the light that streamed in from the windows. Every time Hogan touched it, he was afraid to break it, even though he knew eggs were sturdier than they looked. He couldn't resist the urge to stroke his fingertips over it, smiling as he did so. "What did you and your dad do today?" he murmured.

When he looked up, Cain was staring at him, a forkful of pie hovering in front of his mouth. Hogan felt his cheeks flush and looked away, thankful his dark color meant that Cain couldn't see he was embarrassed. "What?" he asked.

Cain shook his head and put down the fork and plate. He leaned closer, and Hogan held his breath. Was Cain about to kiss him? It certainly looked like it when Cain moved even closer.

Hogan held his breath. He was afraid to move and break

the moment, and he really fucking wanted Cain to kiss him.

A knock on the door interrupted them.

Hogan groaned and flopped back into the nest.

Cain chuckled and rose to his feet, heading toward the door.

Hogan was tempted to tell him not to open, but he knew better. It could be one of his other parents, jealous that Freya had met Cain and they hadn't.

Cain opened the door. "Blake. We were just about to head out for dinner," he said. He stepped aside, but Blake didn't come in.

"No time for dinner. Morven is laying his egg."

Hogan shot to his feet. Now that he knew what laying an egg meant, he realized that Morven wouldn't need any of them. He could probably have done with just Sheldon, but Sheldon had refused in case something went wrong. That meant a healer would be there, and Hogan—and he was pretty sure every single one of their group of friends—was glad. No one knew what would happen to the baby, since they would be a human and dragon hybrid. This was Morven's first pregnancy, so he couldn't even say if it felt normal.

They all wanted to be there for him and Sheldon. This was the one occasion in which Hogan's fists couldn't solve the problem, and he loathed that. He wanted to do so much more. He wanted to tell Morven and Sheldon everything would be okay and that their baby would be perfect.

He couldn't.

He could be there for his friends, though, so he grabbed the egg, not even bothering with a harness, and moved toward the door. Cain and Blake were waiting for him, and as soon as the door was closed behind him, they headed toward Morven and Sheldon's rooms.

Hogan's mouth was dry. No one knew what would

happen, or even if the baby would be in an egg. Hogan suspected they would, but how could he know? There was no way for anyone to be sure if the baby and Morven would make it, and the thought that they might not made Hogan want to punch the wall.

He wouldn't. He and the others were there for support, even though it meant he couldn't stab anyone with his fork. He didn't know if he would be enough support, since punching people was the only thing he could do, but he would try. Morven needed him, and he was one of Hogan's best friends. Whatever Hogan could do for him in this situation, he would.

He just prayed he wouldn't have to do anything he wasn't ready for and that everything would be okay.

Even as they rushed toward Morven and Sheldon's rooms, Cain couldn't help but wonder if Hogan would have pushed him away. He'd been about to kiss him, unable to resist the urge anymore.

He'd been watching Hogan with the egg. Cain talked to his egg, even though it was a one-way conversation. No one knew what the baby dragons could feel in the egg, although a lot of people were convinced that they could hear their parents and recognize their voices eventually. That was one of the reasons Cain talked to his egg. The other was that he loved it, even though it hadn't hatched yet, and he wanted his baby to feel like part of the family right from the beginning.

He was the only one who talked to his egg, though. No one else in their group of friends had tried, and it made sense. They didn't have the connection Cain had with it.

Hogan did. Cain hadn't expected him to talk to the egg, and he'd been stunned. He also understood what it meant. It wasn't just an egg for Hogan, just like it wasn't for Cain. It was already a baby, someone they loved, and Hogan had shown it. *That* had made Cain decide to throw caution to the wind and kiss him, but they'd been interrupted. Now that he knew why, he couldn't find it in himself to be sorry. There would be plenty of time for him to kiss Hogan, but Morven would be laying his first egg only once. Morven needed them, and they would be there for him.

Cain was the only one in their group who had gone through laying an egg, but he hoped Morven wouldn't need him. His experience had been far from normal, and Morven's wouldn't be, either. Cain had laid his egg while on the run, only helped by Hogan, while Morven was laying the first human and dragon hybrid anyone could remember. Cain found himself panicking if he thought about everything that could go wrong, so he tried to focus on what could go right instead.

Whatever the baby would look like, Sheldon and Morven would love them. It didn't matter to them that the baby was a hybrid. It was their baby. That wasn't going to change today or the day the egg hatched.

That wasn't the main worry everyone had, though. What if dragons and humans couldn't have children together? Everyone had been holding their breath as Morven's pregnancy progressed. Cain suspected at least a few in their group had wondered if Morven would manage to bring it to term and lay the egg. As far as Cain was aware, all the healers Morven had gone to had said that the pregnancy was progressing normally, which gave them hope.

Cain prayed that hope wouldn't be quashed tonight.

They finally reached Sheldon and Morven's rooms. Orran, Octavia, and Slavin were already outside, waiting, while the door behind them was closed.

"What's going on?" Hogan asked once they reached them.

They didn't even look surprised to see Hogan holding Cain's egg. "So far, nothing new," Slavin said.

"Has anyone tried to go in?"

"Of course not. We're giving the fathers and the healer space. Our place is out here, not in there with them."

Hogan huffed. "I'm aware of that. I'm just worried."

"We all are."

They settled down to wait. There was no way to know how long it would take for Morven to lay his egg, but Cain remembered well when it had happened to him. He didn't know what he would have done without Hogan, and he was grateful he hadn't had to find out.

"What do you think is happening?" Blake asked.

"I don't know," Orran answered. "I've never laid an egg. You should ask Cain."

Everyone turned to him, and Cain sighed. He didn't particularly want to talk about it, but he understood why Blake was asking. "It's painful," he explained. "There's no way around that, no matter how much I wish there was. The contractions . . . they're the worst pain I've ever felt."

Blake grimaced. "Why would you want to go through that, then?"

Cain looked at Hogan and the egg. He couldn't help but smile. "Because it's worth it. I remembered the pain, but laying your egg and knowing that you're a father makes all of it disappear. I can't wait to meet my baby, and I know they wouldn't be here if I hadn't gone through that." He also wouldn't have met Hogan.

No matter what happened next, he would never regret that.

"Do you think Morven and the baby will be okay?" Blake's voice was soft and vulnerable.

Those were his brother's love and baby. If something happened to them, it would break Sheldon and Blake's hearts. Blake didn't want his brother to be hurt, but there was nothing he could do. There was nothing any of them could do, and even though Cain understood that, it made him angsty. Like

Hogan earlier, he wanted to barge in and do everything he could to help, but since there was no possibility of that happening, he leaned against the wall.

He was grateful Blake didn't ask any more questions. It had been hard to talk while also worrying about Morven, but now that silence had settled on them, he kind of missed Blake's voice. The conversation had been a welcome distraction, and without it, he couldn't avoid focusing on the sounds coming from the room behind them.

He closed his eyes. He recognized the grunting, the cries of pain. He could hear the soothing sounds of Sheldon's voice, and he imagined Sheldon was holding Morven's hand, talking him through the pain and the laying. Unfortunately, Cain knew it didn't help much. Or maybe that was because he and Hogan hadn't known each other when Cain had laid his egg. Maybe having Sheldon there was helping Morven more than Hogan's presence had for Cain. Maybe the feelings between them made all the difference.

Cain doubted that was the case, but he still hoped it was for Morven.

They waited. None of them were hungry anymore, so they stayed in the hallway, listening to what was going on. A few dragons passed them in the hallway, but thankfully, none of them stopped to ask what was going on. Cain was pretty sure Hogan would have snapped if they had, and they would have found themselves with one or two black eyes.

When the door finally opened, they all rushed toward it. The healer walked out, looking tired, but she was smiling, and that gave Cain hope. She was the healer who had examined him when he'd first arrived, and he trusted her. She'd been nothing but nice to him, and more importantly, reassuring.

"How are they?" Blake asked.

The healer's smile widened. "Both the father and egg are perfect. They're resting now."

Cain's chest felt like it caved in with relief. "So the egg is fine?" he asked.

The healer nodded. "It looks perfectly normal." She hesitated. "Of course, we don't know what the baby will be like, but this is a good sign. Sheldon's humanity didn't change the pregnancy, which gives me hope for the baby."

"Can we see them?" Hogan asked.

"Sheldon and Morven are waiting for you."

She walked away, and Cain looked at the others. He could wait outside while they went in since he'd been part of their group for much less time. Morven and Sheldon would want to see their family, and he wasn't sure he was part of it yet.

But as Hogan moved toward the door to step in, he grabbed Cain's hand and dragged him along while he held Cain's egg to his chest with the other hand. Cain couldn't resist, so he didn't. He wanted to make sure Morven and the egg were okay with his own two eyes.

It was easy to find Morven and Sheldon. Both of them were curled in their nest, Morven in his human form. The egg was between them, and Cain held his breath as he stepped closer.

He hadn't known what to expect since Sheldon was human, but the egg truly looked normal. It was a light green, much lighter than Morven's skin, which makes sense since the egg was half-human. It looked exactly the way a dragon egg should look, and for the first time since Blake had knocked on the door, Cain truly relaxed.

Everything would be okay. He had to believe that, and so did Morven and Sheldon.

Watching Cain, Hogan wondered if Cain might want to have more children one day. Hell, it made him wonder if *he* would want children one day. He couldn't imagine himself getting pregnant, but maybe that was because he'd never thought about it seriously. It had never been a concrete possibility, but he felt like he and Cain were on the brink of something big, something that could last a lifetime, and he didn't want to ruin everything by not keeping his mind open.

Hogan couldn't see himself pregnant. He supposed that no one could see it until they got pregnant, so maybe it was something he should keep in mind. Or maybe not. If Cain wanted other children, he might want to be the one to carry them and lay the egg. All of this was so far out in the future that Hogan would go nuts if he obsessed over it, so he focused on what he was currently doing.

This was only the second egg Hogan had seen from up close, and he carefully moved toward the nest. Sheldon and Morven looked like they were in heaven. Morven also looked tired, but Hogan would have been surprised if he hadn't.

"How are you feeling?" Octavia asked as she crouched next to the nest.

"As if I slammed against a mountain while flying," Morven answered.

There was a hint of humor in his voice, thankfully, and Hogan relaxed. Everything truly had gone all right. Morven and the egg were both okay, and there was nothing anyone could do but wait.

While everyone else was focused on Sheldon and Morven, Hogan knelt by the nest and stroked a finger down the length of the egg. It felt like Cain's, even though it appeared different. They were both a pale color, though, and this was starting to feel familiar.

Hogan splayed his fingers on the surface, smiling when he thought about the baby dragon forming inside. "You're going to make your fathers so happy," he murmured.

When he looked up, he found Morven staring at him. He scrambled back as if he'd been caught doing something he shouldn't have, and maybe he had. Cain didn't have a problem with Hogan touching his egg or talking to it, but this wasn't Cain's egg. Hogan should have remembered that.

But instead of being angry, Morven smiled. "You're going to be a good father," he murmured.

Hogan shook his head. "I'm not planning on having children anytime soon."

Morven arched a brow. "You do remember what we talked about in the dining room the other day, right? You're already a father. Cain's egg might not have hatched yet, but it will soon, and everyone here knows you'll be right there with Cain when it does."

Hogan had realized he was kind of obvious, at least to his friends. He didn't like it. It wasn't like he wanted everyone to think he didn't have feelings, but he didn't like being vulnerable. That was when bad things happened, and he didn't want bad things to happen to him. Besides, he had no way to know what Cain wanted except by asking, and even though it made him feel like a coward, he wasn't ready to do that.

He was pretty sure that Cain had been about to kiss him earlier before Blake had come knocking on their door. He knew what he would have done if Cain had.

He would have kissed him back.

He yearned for it, and he wanted to take the next step, but he also didn't want to take advantage of Cain. He realized how strange their relationship and their situation was. Cain felt grateful because Hogan had been there when no one else had been. He'd helped Cain lay his first egg, and of course that kind of situation linked people together, whether or not they were willing. In the beginning, Hogan hadn't wanted to be linked to Cain, but he wasn't angry about it anymore. He liked Cain, and besides, that feeling of being pulled into something he didn't want had only lasted a few moments.

Like Morven had said, Hogan had to decide whether or not he was in this for the long run, and he was. The only question now was what the next step would be. Should he give Cain space? Or should he push gently and see where things went?

"Not to offend anyone, but we'd really like some time to rest," Sheldon said.

Everyone scrambled to their feet. Hogan was still holding Cain's egg, and he pressed it against his chest, needing to feel the smooth heaviness of it. Like always, it made him realize he wasn't alone anymore. He didn't know how or why it had happened, but whatever the future held, he would always be there for Cain and his baby. Whether or not he could be another father for the egg was an entirely different problem, but it was easy to care for it for now. It gave Hogan time to focus on Cain and what they both wanted to happen next.

"You're taking at least a few weeks off, aren't you?" Hogan asked as he and the others moved toward the door.

Sheldon snorted, but it was Morven who answered. "Maybe tomorrow, but there's no reason for me to take more days off work."

Hogan glared at him. "You just laid your first egg. No one will care if you come to work. You should rest and spend some time bonding with the egg."

"I can do that while also working. You have, after all."

Hogan couldn't deny that. Sometimes, when Cain went flying or wanted some time with their friends, Hogan took care of the egg. He'd taken it to work more than once, always happy and proud to show it off. He *was* acting like a father, wasn't he? He hadn't realized it, and now that he did, he wasn't quite sure what to do with it.

"Besides, it's better if Morven takes time off when the egg hatches," Sheldon continued. "That's when I'll need help to deal with the baby and when we should focus on them."

He wasn't wrong. Still, Hogan didn't like it. He knew how tiring laying an egg could be from spending time with Cain after he'd done it. Morven deserved more than a day of rest.

But Morven was his own boss, and no one would be able to force him to take time off. Hogan made a mental note to keep a special eye on him, just in case, but he didn't bring it up again.

He and the others finally left. It was late, and they didn't cross anyone else in the hallways.

"Do you think there's something left to eat in the kitchen?" Slavin asked.

"I'm sure there is," Octavia answered. She looked at the rest of their group. "How about we have a midnight snack?"

Hogan didn't know if it was midnight, but he was hungry, and he needed to feed Cain, so he nodded. They made their way to the kitchen, with Hogan and Cain bringing up the rear. Hogan leaned closer, wanting to talk to Cain on his own. "Are you okay?" he asked.

Cain frowned. "Why wouldn't I be?"

"I know your laying wasn't easy, and I didn't want what happened tonight to remind you of it."

Cain's frown turned into a smile. "It did remind me of it, but it's not a bad thing. My laying was nothing like I expected it to be, but only because it was better. I thought I would be entirely alone, and I was terrified that if something went wrong, I wouldn't have help. Instead, you were there with me, and I wouldn't change that for anything in the world. It also reminded me that soon, we'll have a baby. I can't stop thinking about that now."

Hogan didn't miss the way Cain had said *we*. He was including Hogan in his future, which was all Hogan needed. Maybe now wasn't the best time for them to get together, but Hogan would be part of Cain's future, and it was all he wanted. He could always have more later.

For now, he was content with what they shared. Once things calmed down, hopefully before the egg hatched, they would talk. Even if they didn't, or Cain wasn't ready for more,

Hogan wasn't going anywhere. He and Cain would have a chance to be together eventually, and he couldn't wait.

CHAPTER FIVE

Cain peered at the eggs, a smile on his face. There wasn't much to do when you were babysitting two eggs, but he didn't mind. He'd been watching his own egg for a while now, and adding Morven's didn't change anything. It wasn't like Cain had a job to do anyway. He knew that eventually he would have to find one, and he was fine with that. The Ogorth clan gave new parents all the time they needed to get used to having a child, including time off between the end of the pregnancy and the egg's hatching. Cain would have the opportunity he needed to bond with his baby before he had to start working.

A screech made him jump. He turned to look at Blake and Blue, who were playing on the floor. The baby was always loud, but especially so when he was playing, which made sense. Every time Cain spent time with him, his thoughts went to his future and when he would have his own baby. He could imagine himself playing around with them on the floor like Blake and Blue were doing now.

Cain's future was rosy, and he was ever so grateful for that.

He realized how lucky he'd been. Anyone else would probably still have been alone in the woods, caring for their egg on their own. He still didn't know what he'd done to earn himself a place in Hogan's life and with the Ogorth clan, but he would never do anything that would risk that. For the first time since he could remember, he was happy.

He wanted more. He wished he and Hogan were closer, or rather that their relationship was different. He supposed they were already as close as family could be, but that didn't stop the yearning he felt for Hogan. Now that he'd taken some time to dwell on his feelings, he realized that the way he felt had nothing to do with being grateful. He was, and he always would be, but there was so much more to this, and he wished he knew how to explain that to Hogan.

Blake suddenly flopped onto the couch next to Cain, and Cain realized he hadn't been paying attention for at least a few minutes.

Blake's face was red and he was sweating slightly, but he was beaming. "Thinking about Hogan?" he teased.

Cain shrugged. He didn't mind the teasing, especially not when it came to this topic. He was pretty sure everyone in their little group knew he was half in love with Hogan and that they were betting on how long it would take him and Hogan to get together.

"Want to talk about it?" Blake asked.

"Weren't you busy with Blue?"

Blake waved. "He's about to get some food, and he'll sleep after that. I have some time. Besides, you look like you need to talk to someone. Not that I'm saying you should talk to me, but if you need to, I'm here."

That was new, too. Back with the Eiloren clan, Cain hadn't had friends. He didn't think any member of the clan had because that wasn't how they did things. The king and most people there didn't care about friendships. They only cared about doing their job and keeping the clan safe and strong, and while Cain understood, now that he'd spent time with the Ogorth clan, he knew friendships weren't frivolous. They were a fundamental part of the clan and what it stood for, and he thought it made the clan even stronger.

There was also the fact that he really liked both Blake and Sheldon, as well as everyone else in their little group. He'd never imagined he would have a family, but he did, and even though sometimes it was overwhelming, he wouldn't give it up for anything in the world.

"I wasn't thinking about Hogan, or at least not entirely. I was just thinking how lucky I've been," Cain murmured.

"You were, but then, I guess the three of us have been. I'm pretty sure I would be dead right now if Orran and his friends hadn't intervened when I stole Blue's egg from my boss. And Sheldon would also be dead if we hadn't intervened after my boss captured him. We both owe a lot to the clan, and so do you."

Cain had never thought about that, but Blake was right. "How was it? When you fell in love with Orran, I mean?"

Blake's gaze lingered on the baby dragon still rolling on the floor. "It was strange. I didn't know dragons were shapeshifters, and in the beginning, I was sure Orran would eat me eventually. I didn't want to give him the egg because I didn't trust he would keep it safe. I had no way to know back then. But we made our way here, and as we did so, I got to know him. This is nothing like I expected my life to be like, but you know what? It's even better."

Cain slowly nodded. "Hogan and I are friends."

"You want more?"

"I do. I'm not sure Hogan does, though." Cain wanted to believe Hogan would have allowed him to kiss him the other night, but he hadn't tried again, and neither had Hogan. Cain wasn't sure what to make of that or what his next step should be.

Maybe it would be better for both him and Hogan if he kept his distance. Even though his feelings had nothing to do with being grateful, he realized that his presence in Hogan's life had flipped it upside down. Hogan had gone from being on his own to having Cain and the egg, and it was a lot to deal with.

Blake tapped his fingertips on his thigh. He was wearing

jeans and a t-shirt, and Cain had to resist the urge to reach for the fabric. He was fascinated by clothes, and even though he understood why it would be stupid for him to wear them, he kind of wanted to. He enjoyed the difference between the fabrics and the way they moved along with Blake's body. He couldn't help but wonder what they would feel like against his skin.

Or maybe against Hogan's.

The thought made him shiver, and he hoped he managed to hide it. He wasn't sure he had when Blake grinned at him, but thankfully, Blake's expression turned serious only seconds later.

"I'm pretty sure Hogan is in love with you," he said. "But we're not close, or at least, not as close as he and Morven are. I always thought that Hogan resented me for being human, but I realized that wasn't the case. He resented me for taking his friend away, and it took him a while to wrap his mind around it and get used to my presence. I think that's Hogan's problem even in this situation. He doesn't like changes, and you were a huge one. He's probably still trying to find his footing, and it's good that you're giving him time. Besides, he's always been okay with your presence in his life. I think that's a big hint that he very much wants more."

Cain hadn't known Hogan had been wary of Blake and Sheldon, although now that he did, it made sense. Blake was right—Hogan didn't like changes, and having Cain and the egg in his life was a big one.

But knowing this gave Cain hope. His egg would hatch soon, and that would be an even bigger change. Maybe now wasn't the time to take a step forward in his relationship with Hogan. If things continued going the way they were, though, he and Hogan would have time to talk and get together. They weren't in a rush, or at least, Cain wasn't. He wanted to enjoy this new life of his, and while that included being with Hogan, it wasn't necessary.

Cain already had so much. Wanting more from Hogan almost felt like asking for too much, and that was something else he had to deal with. He and Hogan both came with a past, and it was a past they needed to accept as well as understand how it influenced their life now.

Once they did, their relationship would be even stronger, which was all Cain wanted.

"I can't believe you're already back at work," Hogan grumbled.

He was pretty sure Morven rolled his eyes, but Morven was leaning toward a screen, watching it instead of Hogan, so it could have been something else. "I already told you I don't need time off, not right now. I'd rather have it once the egg hatches."

"You're the boss. You could take time off both now and then."

Morven straightened and turned to Hogan. "I'm not sure if you love me that much or if you have your eyes on my job and want me out of the way."

Hogan shuddered in horror. "I don't want your job. I didn't even want *this* job, but I can't give it up."

Morven's gaze was knowing. "Because of Cain and the baby."

Hogan nodded curtly. He didn't want to say it out loud, and besides, Morven already knew all about this. "You can keep your job, and I'll keep mine. I'm just worried about you. I remember all too well when Cain laid his egg, and it's too soon for you to be back at work."

"But Cain laid his egg alone in the forest."

"What am I, chopped liver?"

Morven chuckled. "No, but you're not a healer. You did

everything you could, and thankfully, both the egg and Cain are okay. It makes sense that he was more tired, though, especially when you consider everything else. He'd been running for part of the night, and he was nervous and anxious. He had to recuperate from that as much as he did from the laying. I didn't have any of those problems. I laid the egg in my nest, with a healer there. I'm perfectly fine, so you can stop worrying."

Hogan doubted he ever would. He cared about his friends, and he didn't think that was a problem.

"We have a message coming in," someone in the room said.

Hogan looked around the security room. He wasn't crazy about this place, even though he realized it was a necessary evil. It was too small, too crowded with computers and dragons. Even though some of them were in their human form, it still felt like it was closing around Hogan, which made him want to run away screaming.

Or maybe he wanted to run to Cain.

"What kind of message?" Morven asked as he moved toward the dragon who'd spoken.

"It comes from outside. It's not one of ours, so probably from another clan." She narrowed her eyes and stared at the screen.

Hogan had no idea how computers worked, but he didn't need to. Thankfully, other people could do that for him.

"It's from the Eiloren clan," the dragon said.

Hogan's back went ramrod straight. He and Morven looked at each other. They both knew what it meant. The Eiloren clan had found out that Cain was with the Ogorth clan, and they weren't happy.

This was Hogan's worst nightmare, but he tried to calm himself by thinking about the fact that no matter what happened, he would protect Cain. He was ready to do anything to help him and keep him here, but if he couldn't, he was also ready to leave with him.

A hand landed on Hogan's shoulder, making him jump.

It was only Morven, who squeezed and leaned closer. "Don't panic," he murmured.

"How can I not? We both know what's going on."

"We don't. Let's see what happens first."

Together, they moved to Sheldon, who was sitting at the back of the room. The computer in front of him illuminated his worried expression. While any dragons in the room could have shown Hogan and Morven the message, Hogan was relieved it would be Sheldon. He, better than any dragon, understood how big this problem could be. Hogan supposed it made sense, since Cain was their friend, while he was only an outsider to most of the clan.

"Show us?" Morven asked.

Sheldon nodded and clicked a few things on the screen. One of the windows widened, showing them a dragon in their human form sitting in a chair. "This isn't a message. They want to talk to us right now."

Hogan almost panicked. He wanted to run to Cain, grab him, and hide him from the world so no one would be able to take him away. He needed to know what was going on so he could protect Cain, though, so he stayed right where he was. "Should we call the queen?" he asked. His voice was rough and growly, even more than usual.

Morven shook his head. "Not yet. I want to see what's going on first, and I have the authority to answer for her."

Sheldon rolled his chair to the side while Morven grabbed another one from a desk nearby. He settled in front of the screen, and once again, Sheldon clicked around the screen. When Morven nodded at him, he nodded back, then suddenly, the dragon on the screen came to life.

"My name is Morven, and I'm head of security for the Ogorth clan," Morven said.

The dragon nodded. "I'm Gerda, head of communications for the Eiloren clan. My king would like to talk to your queen."

"What is this about?"

Relationships and communications between clans were often tense. They always had been, although with the humans being such a danger to dragons, a lot of the clans had started working together, or at the very least, they'd agreed not to attack each other. But it didn't take much to burn that agreement to the ground, and the Ogorth clan sheltering a runaway member of the Eiloren clan could certainly create trouble.

Gerda looked sideways, gave a tiny nod, and turned her attention back to Morven. "We were made aware of the fact that you're holding one of our clan members."

"We're not holding anyone."

"That you're sheltering him, then. We would like him and his egg back."

"I imagine that if Cain wanted to go back to his old clan, he already would have. He's happy with us, which means he's not going anywhere. I'm sorry, but I can't help you."

Morven's tone and words were normal, but Hogan could see the tension in his back. That made him even more nervous. Was Morven angry on Cain's behalf, or was he worried about what was about to happen?

It had been a long time since the Ogorth clan had gone to war with another clan. No one wanted to see the destruction and loss of life that would result from something like that, not even Hogan. He imagined that if Morven and the queen had to choose between keeping the clan safe and keeping Cain with them, they would choose the clan. It wouldn't be easy for them, but it would make sense. They needed to protect every single clan member, and the safety of one dragon couldn't hold up against that.

Hogan didn't have to follow the same rules. He could focus

on keeping Cain safe, and he would if he had to, no matter what it entailed.

Gerda linked their fingers together. "I'm sure you understand why this is a problem. Cain is one of our clan members, and he belongs with us."

"From what he told me, you didn't treat him like a clan member, but rather, like a servant."

Gerda looked offended for a moment, but she smoothed her expression. "The way we organize our clan has nothing to do with you, and we don't need your opinion on it. Whatever happened, Cain shouldn't have left, especially not taking one of our eggs with him. He's a runaway, and we *demand* him back."

Insisting with his refusal wouldn't help Morven or the Ogorth clan. Even Hogan could see that, and he wasn't diplomatic in the least. They had to be smart about it, which didn't come easy to Hogan. Thankfully for him, Morven knew what he was doing.

"You understand I'll have to talk to my queen about this."

Gerda didn't look happy, but she nodded. "Of course. We'll be waiting for news from you. Just understand that there's only one outcome that will satisfy us. We want Cain and our egg back, and nothing else will be acceptable."

Morven looked at Sheldon and nodded. Gerda's image disappeared from the screen, and Hogan finally allowed himself to relax. Then, he started panicking.

When the door opened and Hogan walked through, Cain couldn't stop the smile that bloomed on his face. He didn't try to hide it, either. He wanted Hogan to know how happy he was to see him.

But Hogan didn't look happy to see *him*. He didn't smile back like he usually did, and Cain dropped his smile and frowned. Something was going on. He was sure of it when Morven stepped in behind Hogan, and both of them shared a dire expression.

Cain straightened and reached for his egg. It was an automatic gesture, something he knew everyone in the room had noticed. It wasn't that he didn't trust them, but he was very much aware of how wrong things could go, and his priority, if anything happened, was to save his egg.

"What is it?" Blake asked as he scrambled to his feet.

Cain didn't miss the way he placed himself in front of him. It was almost as if Blake was trying to protect him, and the feelings the gesture created in Cain were almost enough to make him cry. He didn't want Blake to fight with anyone, not when he needed a place with the Ogorth clan even more than Cain.

He rose to his feet and touched Blake's back. "It's okay. They're friends. They won't do anything to hurt me."

Blake stared at Cain for a second before nodding and stepping away. "I still want to know what's going on," he said.

"Where's Blue?" Morven asked.

"In bed. He fell asleep about half an hour ago. You can talk."

Morven nodded. He wasn't who Cain was looking at, though. Cain's gaze was on Hogan as he waited, holding his breath.

Hogan rubbed his face. "We were just contacted by the Eiloren clan."

The world tilted around again. He reached back, needing to sit down. He managed to get to the couch and not drop his egg, and he cradled it to his chest, needing the reassurance that it was still there with him.

He'd known something like this could happen and that it probably would. But it had been weeks since he'd left the Eiloren clan, and he supposed he'd started fooling himself that he was safe and that they wouldn't find him. Clearly, he was wrong, and he knew what they wanted. "I'm not giving them my egg," he said through gritted teeth.

"No one asked you to," Morven said. "But it *is* what they want. You and the egg, and they won't accept anything else. The queen wants to talk to you."

It was hard not to panic. The only times Cain had seen the queen had been the first day after he'd arrived and when she'd confirmed he was an Ogorth clan member. He'd been happy, and he still was, but he knew that if she had to choose, she would choose the clan over him. He wouldn't berate her for it. The clan was her priority as the queen, while he was just a recent member.

Hogan crouched in front of Cain and took one of his hands. "I know it's hard, but I promise nothing will happen to you."

Cain shook his head. "You can't make that kind of promise. You don't know what's going to happen."

"You're right. I can't know for sure, but I *can* promise that I'll be next to you for as long as you need and want me to. That includes running away, if that's what's needed."

Cain shook his head. Hogan had promised that when they'd met, too, but Cain had a hard time believing it. "You can't give up your home for me."

Hogan's expression was fierce. "Watch me. I'm not giving *you* up, Cain. I'm not allowing anyone to give you back to the Eiloren clan, and I'll do everything I can so it doesn't happen. They'll have to walk over my dead body."

Morven cleared his throat. "Let's not go there just yet. We don't know what will happen, but the queen needs to talk to you, Cain. You can leave your egg here with Blake. He'll take care of it."

Cain didn't want to do it, but he trusted Blake. Blake wouldn't be able to stand up to guards if they came to get the egg, but then, neither would Cain. It wouldn't make sense for him to take his egg in for a meeting with the queen, and maybe, if he was lucky, Blake would be able to hide the egg if something happened.

Cain got to his feet. His legs shook, and he felt like if he tried taking a step forward, he would fall. Thankfully, Hogan was there, like always, supporting Cain and helping him.

Cain swallowed. "I'm ready to go."

"I promise I'll keep your egg safe," Blake said.

He sounded worried and angry, and even though Cain hated this situation, that was good to hear. Blake cared about him, and he wasn't the only one. Cain had to remember that he wasn't alone anymore. He had people who would fight for him and his baby.

Hogan stayed close as he and Cain followed Morven to the throne room. Cain wondered what was about to happen. Would the queen ask her guards to grab him right away? Or would he be allowed back to Hogan's rooms? If he was, if he managed to get back to his egg, there was a chance he could run. He couldn't ask Hogan to give up his entire life for him, but that didn't mean he couldn't run away. He'd managed to escape the Eiloren clan once. He could do it again.

"Don't do anything stupid," Hogan murmured. "And trust me. I'll die protecting you if it comes to that."

"I don't want you to die. I don't want anyone to be hurt because of me." But if he didn't go back, someone would. There was no way out of it.

Cain was ready to run away by the time they reached the throne room. Morven pushed open the doors, and Cain felt trapped as he followed him inside. The queen had been nice to him, but he wouldn't be surprised if she wasn't anymore. She had her clan to protect, and it was more important than Cain.

She was in her human form when they arrived, which surprised Cain. It probably showed in his expression, because she smiled. "With Sheldon and Blake with us, more dragons are starting to spend time in their human form," she explained. "I thought it would be a good example if I did, too. It's one of the reasons I wanted Blake and Sheldon with us, after all."

Cain nodded. It had become a habit for him, too, because of how much time he spent with Sheldon and Blake.

"Now on to the problem," the queen continued. "I'm sure Morven and Hogan have told you what happened."

Cain's mouth was dry. "The Eiloren clan found out I was here. They want me and my egg back."

The queen nodded. Her expression was soft, and Cain thought he saw pity in her eyes. "That's what they're asking for, yes. I'm sure you understand what could happen if I don't go along with this."

"They could attack the Ogorth clan. It would mean life losses for you, and it's not something you want." Cain didn't, either. Most of the Ogorth clan dragons had been welcoming, if a bit wary. Cain didn't blame them, and he'd been looking forward to getting to know the clan.

"You can't hand him over to them," Hogan suddenly said. "I understand why this is a problem for you, but if you decide to go along with this, Cain and I will leave. Maybe you can say that you had no idea we were planning that. It should keep them away from the clan while also helping Cain."

Cain wasn't surprised by Hogan's words, but he wished he hadn't said them. Now he'd exposed both himself and Cain, and it would be harder for them to run away if they had to.

The queen's eyes had widened, and she was staring at Hogan. "You would do that for him? You'd leave your clan, your family, and your friends?"

Cain held his breath in anticipation, but he shouldn't have.

"I would. I wouldn't be happy about it, but this isn't fair. The Eiloren clan wants to take Cain's egg away from him.

They were treating him and who knows how many others as servants instead of clan members. Who wouldn't want a better life? Who wouldn't want to keep their baby and watch them grow? As far as I'm concerned, he did the only thing he could, and I'll do everything I can to make sure he stays free and can raise his child."

The queen slowly nodded. "I see. I hadn't realized the two of you were so close, although maybe I should have. But you won't have to run away with him. Everything you said is right. I don't have a say in how the Eiloren clan is run, but every member should be allowed to leave if they want to, just like they are in our clan. Besides, Cain is an Ogorth clan member now. It's my duty to protect him, just like I would protect every other member."

Cain wondered if he was still breathing. It didn't feel like it.

The queen looked at him. "I'm not saying it'll be easy, and I'm worried about what the Eiloren clan is ready to do. We need to talk about that, and about a lot of other things. But I want you to know that as far as I'm concerned, you won't be going back to them. *This* is your home now, and I'll protect you and the clan as well as I can."

Cain's knees buckled, and he was pretty sure he would have hit the floor if Hogan hadn't been there to keep him on his feet. Hogan wrapped an arm around Cain's waist, pulling him close, and Cain didn't hesitate to press himself against him and hug him back. They'd never done this, and maybe they weren't ready to do it, but he needed support.

He needed Hogan.

For a moment, Hogan really had thought the queen would sacrifice Cain for the sake of the clan. He wouldn't have blamed her, and he would have understood, but he also would have done everything he could to keep Cain safe.

He wouldn't have to.

If he was honest with himself, he didn't want to leave his family behind. No matter how annoying his parents were, they were still his parents, and he loved them as much as they loved him. He wanted to give that to Cain and Cain's baby. They didn't have any family with the Ogorth clan, but they could have Hogan's. Hogan was glad he and Cain wouldn't have to leave, although that didn't solve the problem of the Eiloren clan creating trouble.

"You should take him back to your rooms," the queen said, looking at Hogan.

Hogan was still holding Cain up, and he could feel how much Cain was trembling. He'd no doubt expected to be handed over to the Eiloren clan, just like Hogan had. This had to be a surprise for him, and even though it was a good one, he was still in shock.

"What about the Eiloren clan?" Morven asked.

The queen sighed. "Why don't you stay with me? We can talk about it. We should probably ask Orran to come, too."

"Then maybe Cain and I should stay," Hogan said.

The queen shook her head. "I know you want to be involved, and I don't have a problem with that. I don't think you or Cain are up to having this conversation right now, though."

She wasn't wrong when it came to Cain, but Hogan wasn't in shock like him. "I could take him home and come back."

Cain shuddered in Hogan's arms, and Hogan knew he wouldn't do it, even if the queen agreed. It was a stupid idea, because he couldn't stay away from Cain, especially not in this kind of situation.

"Stay with him. He needs you, now more than ever," she said. "I promise we'll keep you up to date. I know how important this is both to you and Cain, and it is to Morven and me, too. You'll be the first to know how we decide to deal with this. I promise."

No matter how much Hogan wanted to push, he knew better. The queen had spoken, and she wouldn't change her mind. Besides, she wasn't wrong. Cain did need Hogan, so Hogan had better focus on that rather than on something he couldn't change right now.

They left Morven in the throne room with the queen and headed to Blue's rooms. Even though he hadn't asked, Hogan didn't think Cain would be able to rest until he had his egg with him. Hogan wasn't going to ask him to try, so instead, they stopped to pick up the egg before heading back to their rooms.

Once there, Hogan guided Cain and the egg to the nest. He made sure the door was locked and that no one would interrupt them, then he slipped into the nest with them. He kept his distance because he wanted Cain to feel as comfortable as possible, but after a while, Cain slid toward him, and Hogan wrapped his arms around him. He kissed the top of Cain's head and closed his eyes.

"Were you really going to leave this place for me?" Cain murmured after a while.

Hogan opened his eyes and looked down at Cain. Cain wasn't looking at him, his arm still tight around his egg, which was pressed between both their stomachs. "I would have."

"It wouldn't have been fair to you, though. This is your home. You shouldn't have to leave it for me."

"You're more important than this place, or even than my family."

Cain finally tilted his head to look at Hogan. "How can you say that? You love your parents and your friends."

Hogan swallowed. This was it, wasn't it? This was the moment he told Cain that he was in love with him and that there was nothing or no one more important to him in the world. His mouth was dry, but Cain needed to understand. Hopefully, it would help him decide to stay.

Because no matter what the queen had said, this wasn't going to be easy. The Eiloren clan wouldn't give up Cain and the egg, which meant the Ogorth clan would have to find a way around that. It would be just like Cain to decide to go back to the Eiloren clan to help the Ogorth clan, and Hogan wanted to make sure Cain wouldn't do something stupid like that.

He swallowed. "I do love my parents and my friends. They're the most important people in the world—right after you. I love you, and I promised to protect you."

Cain propped himself up on one elbow without letting go of the egg with the other arm. "I understand that, but I never expected you to keep that promise in a case like this one. Besides, I might be your friend, but I'm not the only one. It's not fair to push me ahead of the others."

Either he hadn't understood, or he wasn't sure what Hogan was saying. Hogan needed to be clear before Cain worked himself up about something he didn't have to worry about. "When I said I love you, I didn't mean as a friend," Hogan explained.

Cain snapped his mouth shut and stared. "What did you mean, then?" he asked. He sounded hesitant.

Hogan could only tell him the truth. "I meant that I love you the way Morven loves Sheldon. I want you in my life, as a friend if that's what you can give me, but as so much more if it's something you might want, too. I know I'm nowhere close to being what you deserve or what you might want, but if you do agree to this, I promise I will keep you and your baby safe for the rest of my life. That's why I was serious about leaving with you if we need to. I would never have forgiven myself if I hadn't, but more importantly, I don't want you to be on your own ever again."

Cain swallowed.

Hogan focused on the movement of his throat, wondering how it would feel to kiss him there.

"What about the clan?" Cain asked.

Hogan didn't miss the fact that Cain hadn't told him what he wanted. He chose to focus on Cain's question. "What about it?"

"I know the queen said she would keep me safe, but protecting me might mean putting the entire clan in danger. I don't want that to happen."

"I don't think anyone wants it, but the queen was serious. You're a clan member now, and we keep our people safe. Besides, from what I know about the Eiloren clan, they're not fighters. They might make a lot of noise and demands, but it doesn't mean they're going to attack."

For everything that was wrong with the Ogorth clan, there was also something good about them, including the fact that the clan was one of the biggest around. Not every clan member was trained to defend themselves or go to war, but there was safety in numbers, even in numbers that wouldn't be useful in a battle.

Cain sighed. "I just don't want anyone to be hurt because of me."

Hogan couldn't resist and kissed his forehead. "Even if someone did get hurt, it wouldn't be because of you. It would be because of the Eiloren clan and no one else. I realize it's probably not easy for you to believe that, but I'll tell you every day if I need to until you do."

Cain finally smiled. "I don't know what I did to deserve you. When I ran away, I never imagined anything like this happening to me."

"Anything like what?"

Cain's smile widened, and he leaned closer.

Hogan held his breath, wondering if this time, they were

finally going to kiss.

They did. Cain's lips brushed against Hogan's, and Hogan released his breath and kissed him back. He'd been dreaming of this for so long that he wouldn't have been able to say no even if they'd been in public—and he hated being affectionate when others were around to gawk. They weren't, thankfully, so Hogan took his time kissing Cain back, needing this to be the perfect first kiss.

As far as he was concerned, it was.

Cain had almost expected Hogan to push him away. He wouldn't have blamed him, not with all the problems he came with.

Instead, Hogan kissed him back, and for one moment, Cain allowed himself to bask in the sensation. He loved Hogan, and Hogan loved him. That was everything he'd ever wanted in his life—someone to love and who would love him in return. He'd looked for it with his egg's father, but he hadn't found it.

He had now.

The thought of losing everything he'd received since he'd arrived in Ogorth clan territory was terrifying, but there was no way out of it. The only thing he could do was stay here and fight back, and now that he wasn't alone, it felt much easier to do. It wouldn't be a walk in the park, but it didn't mean the situation was doomed.

When Cain pulled away, Hogan stared at him with wide eyes. His lips were slick, and Cain wanted to kiss him again, but they had other things to focus on.

Cain sat up. "I can help the queen and Morven plan. I know the Eiloren clan, and I'll give them as much information as I can."

Instead of going along with it like Cain had expected,

Hogan took his arm and gently pulled him back to the nest. "They have things under control."

"They don't know the Eiloren clan," Cain protested.

"They don't need to right now. The only thing that's going to happen today is that the queen will talk to Gerda, the dragon who talked to Morven earlier. She'll explain that she has no intention of giving you up, and that will put the ball on their side."

"They're dangerous. They could attack, and that won't end well for anyone."

"Do you really think they're going to attack? Because from what I know, they don't have the numbers to go against us."

Cain took a deep breath and forced himself to think through the panic. He didn't want to lose his new home and his family, and to make sure that didn't happen, he had to focus on what he knew about his old clan.

"They don't," he finally agreed.

"You said you know the clan well. What do you think they'll do?"

It was easier to think now that he was focusing on something he could help with, so Cain explained, "The king will try to find another way to get to me and the egg. He has to know it's the only way to get us back. An attack won't work, even if they take the Ogorth clan by surprise. Somehow getting to me and my baby would be better, but that means the Eiloren clan would need a spy here and a way to get in." Cain couldn't imagine any member of the Ogorth clan wanting to betray the queen.

Hogan grimaced. "We're going to have to be careful. I wouldn't be surprised if someone used this situation to get back at the queen. Some people aren't happy about Blake and Sheldon's presence here. This will play in their favor."

Cain had heard about the grumbles, and Blake and Sheldon had explained what was going on. The thought of anyone using the situation against the queen made him want to scream. "So we should keep an eye on that cousin of hers, right?"

"He's the main problem right now. Hopefully, he'll see that helping the Eiloren clan would only put us in danger, but I wouldn't swear on that. He's not the brightest claw on the paw."

"Wouldn't he have to be, if he wants to become king instead?"

Hogan snorted. "Oh, he thinks a lot about himself, but that doesn't mean he's right. He'd already tried twice to get to the queen and topple her off the throne. So far, he hasn't managed, and I think that speaks volumes."

"He might succeed. With Blake and Sheldon, the clan wasn't in danger. This time, you are, and I'm sure that a lot of clan members will go along with whatever he says just to save themselves." And Cain wouldn't blame them. He would sacrifice anyone to save his baby, even people he loved.

"I know that telling you not to worry about him won't help. I truly think that the queen knows what she's doing, though. She'll find a way out of this, and you won't have to worry about the Eiloren clan ever again."

Cain wanted to believe Hogan, but he wasn't sure he could. This entire situation was a mess—a mess he wished he could clean up, but he couldn't. The only thing he could do was wait to see what happened, but the thought of not doing anything to help didn't sit well with him.

What could he do, though?

CHAPTER SIX

Hogan wished he and Cain had gotten together in a different moment. As it was, he felt like he couldn't focus on Cain the way he should be, not with the danger of the Eiloren clan attacking hovering over their heads.

It had been a week, and they hadn't heard from the clan again. Hogan hadn't been there, but both Morven and the queen had told him what had happened. After they'd talked to Cain about the Eiloren clan, the queen had contacted their king, and she'd told him that Cain was staying with the Ogorth clan since he was officially a clan member. She'd made sure he knew that attacking Cain or trying to do anything to hurt him would mean pulling the Ogorth clan in a conflict no one wanted. He hadn't been happy, but he'd retreated—for now.

Hogan wasn't convinced the Eiloren king really had. He wanted to believe the man wouldn't be an idiot and would go along with what the queen wanted, but he knew all too well that some people weren't smart, especially when it came to their wounded pride. Cain had shown the Eiloren clan that the king didn't have the entire clan in hand, that he didn't control every member. The king had to be pissed. Hopefully, that didn't mean he would do something stupid.

There was relief in knowing that the Ogorth clan would protect Cain. Hogan wasn't stupid, and he realized that some clan members would eagerly hand Cain over if they could. Luckily, there were more members who would protect him, both because he was one of them and because they'd be horrified if they knew what the Eiloren clan did.

It was true that children were precious, especially for dragons, but that was one more reason not to take them away from their parents. The Ogorth clan and the queen would never consider taking children away from their parents, let alone not telling them what happened to them. It was madness—a madness Hogan was glad Cain had fled.

Still, not knowing what was going to happen next made everything feel fragile. That was probably why Hogan and Cain were still hesitant around each other as a couple. It was everything Hogan had wanted, but in a way, it also wasn't. They were having a hard time fitting together in a different way than before, but Hogan knew that eventually, it would get better.

It had to.

You know, since you and Cain got together, you've been distracted, Octavia said. Thankfully, she sounded amused rather than offended that Hogan had been ignoring her and Slavin.

I'd be distracted, too, if I was with Cain, Slavin pointed out.

Hogan narrowed his eyes at him. *Why have you been thinking about being with Cain?* he asked.

Slavin rolled his eyes. *You can stop trying to intimidate me. That wasn't what I meant, and you know it. Octavia is right, though. You've been distracted.*

That's not true. It *was* true, but Hogan would never admit it.

Really? What were Octavia and I talking about, then?

Hogan tried to answer, but he couldn't. He'd been thinking about Cain and what was going on with the Eiloren clan. He had no clue what Octavia and Slavin had been saying.

That made him a bad guard. The three of them were on duty in the throne room, which meant they were supposed to be focused on protecting the queen. She wasn't here, though. That was the only reason they were relaxed, but they would be on guard if she walked into the throne room. In the meantime, Hogan had allowed his thoughts to drift, which wasn't good.

He sighed. *Fine. You're right. I was distracted, and it has to do with Cain.*

Slavin's gleeful expression made Hogan want to punch him in the face. That was hard to do when he was in his dragon form, but he could certainly try. He might have if he didn't love Slavin as much as he did.

We were talking about what Morven said about adding a fourth member to our team, Octavia said before Hogan could decide whether or not it would be worth it to hit Slavin.

Hogan couldn't remember having that conversation with Morven, which was a problem. *Why would he want to add a member to our team? Three is the perfect number.*

There were four of us before he got his promotion, Octavia pointed out.

Hogan grumbled. *Fine. Four was the perfect number when he was on the team with us. Now that he isn't, three is. I don't want to have to deal with another team member. No one would be as good as he was.*

Octavia sighed. *I agree with you. I don't want a new team member, but we're probably going to have to get used to the idea. Morven isn't wrong. It would be better if there were four of us working together instead of three, especially with what's going on.* She didn't have to mention the Eiloren clan. Both Slavin and Hogan knew that was who she was talking about.

The door opened, and a dragon peeked in. Hogan moved to place himself in front of them, staring them down. *Yes?* he asked.

The dragon didn't look scared, which was a first, because Hogan usually got that kind of reaction. It probably had to do with his color or with his permanent scowl.

I'd like to talk to the queen. It's urgent, the dragon said.

Hogan nodded. *Your name?*

Lysander.

Hogan frowned. He knew that name, but he couldn't

remember where he'd heard it.

I'll let the queen know, Slavin said, already moving toward the door at the end of the throne room that led to her office.

Lysander stepped in and closed the door. They were a gray dragon, someone most people wouldn't notice. The fact that they wanted to talk to the queen said a lot, though. It meant she knew them, and since whatever they had to tell her was urgent, they were important to her somehow.

Hogan was still trying to remember where he'd heard Lysander's name when the queen came in. She was in her dragon form, too, and instead of climbing onto the throne, she moved toward Lysander.

I didn't expect you to come by this soon, she said.

Lysander looked at Octavia, Slavin, and Hogan. *I have news, but it's important.*

The queen nodded. *You can talk in front of them. I've already called Morven, and he'll be here in a few minutes.*

Are you sure, your Majesty? This is something only a few selected people should know about.

They've been in this since the beginning. Hogan is Cain's partner, and he'll find out about this eventually anyway. You might as well tell him and his friends now. That way, I won't have to repeat whatever you're about to tell us. I trust them with my life, and so should you.

Lysander didn't look impressed, and they stared at Hogan, Slavin, and Octavia for a bit longer than necessary and polite. Ordinarily, Hogan would have snarled at them, but he could feel this truly was important. He'd remembered who Lysander was, or rather, where he'd heard their name.

Lysander was a spy.

After Morven had gotten his promotion, he'd talked to Octavia, Slavin, Hogan, and Orran a lot. He'd wanted them to know what was going on because he trusted them, and because Orran had been in his place once. That meant they'd gone over documents and people they would need to work with, and that included Lysander. The file hadn't said anything about them except for the fact that they were a spy, and Hogan was curious to find out more about them.

There was no doubt in his mind that Lysander was working on the Eiloren clan problem. What that meant, Hogan had no idea, but he supposed he was about to find out. Hopefully, it was good news, but from Lysander's expression, he doubted it. He wanted to ask, but they were waiting for Morven.

When he finally arrived, Hogan could have kissed him. Instead, he stayed where he was, tense and ready to act if it was needed. They all turned toward Lysander, who was standing there as if it was the most natural thing in the world. They looked at ease, but Hogan suspected they weren't, from their shifty eyes. Lysander knew where every exit was, and they probably had about half a dozen plans to get out of the room if anything happened.

When the door closed behind Morven, Lysander straightened. *Is everyone here?* he asked.

The queen nodded. *Yes, and we're listening. What did you find about the Eiloren clan?*

Cain was surprised by a knock on the door. He eyed it, wondering who it could be. Maybe one of Hogan's parents? After the dinner they'd had together, they'd started to come by every so often, usually alone, but sometimes in pairs. It was clear to Cain that they were happy to see Cain was in Hogan's life, as well as the egg. They were already acting like grandparents, something that puzzled Cain but also made him happy.

"You should probably open," Sheldon said.

He was sitting on the couch, both his egg and Cain's by his side. Blake was there, too, watching TV from the floor. They looked at home here, like they belonged, and Cain realized they did. They were his friends, his family, and he was more than happy to spend time with them.

He strode toward the door, opening it and freezing when he saw a guard standing there. He didn't recognize them, and he held his breath, shifting since the guard was in their dragon form.

The guard looked at him. *The queen wants to see you*, they said.

Cade swallowed. *What's going on?* he asked.

I was only told the queen wants to see you. Can you come now?

Cain looked back. Both Sheldon and Blake were staring, but of course, they had no idea what was going on. *Give me a moment*, he told the guard before shifting back to his human form. "The queen wants to see me," he explained.

Sheldon straightened. "What's going on?"

"I don't know. That's all the guard has told me. The queen wants to see me, and I think it's urgent, because she wants to see me *now*."

This was it, wasn't it? The queen had told Cain and Hogan she'd talked to the Eiloren king and had told him she wouldn't hand Cain over. Cain had been relieved, but he'd expected something to happen. The king was probably putting pressure on the queen, and she couldn't avoid giving up Cain anymore. He hoped that she would at least allow the egg to stay with the Ogorth clan, although he suspected that the Eiloren clan was more interested in the egg than in him.

"I can see you worrying, and I don't think you should," Blake said, getting to his feet and moving closer. "The queen has already promised she wouldn't hand you over to your old clan. She won't go back on her word."

Cain rubbed his face. "You can't know that. It would make sense for her to when the clan is in danger."

"But just like she wouldn't hand any other clan member over, she won't do it to you, either. I know you're nervous and anxious. But keep in mind that you have people fighting for you, and they include her."

Cain wasn't convinced, but he nodded. He didn't want Blake and Sheldon to realize how terrified he was. "Can you keep an eye on my egg?"

"You don't even have to ask," Sheldon answered. "We'll take both of them to mine and Morven's room, all right? You can come by once you're done talking to the queen. Take your time if you need it. The egg will be safe with me."

That was all Cain could hope and ask for. He walked Sheldon and Blake out, then watched them stride down the hallway, each of them holding an egg. He wanted to go with them, but instead, he turned to the guard, who was still waiting in the hallway. He shifted back, then nodded. *I'm ready.*

The guard headed down the hallway, and Cain followed them. By the time they reached the throne room, he'd come up with a hundred different ways this meeting could go. Most of them ended up with him being given back to the Eiloren clan, which meant he was ready to run away when he stepped into the room.

The only reason he didn't was that Hogan was there.

Everyone in the room had gathered at the end of it. They were talking quietly, but Hogan looked up when he heard the door, and he rushed toward Cain. Cain was relieved, but that didn't mean he wasn't anxious about what was about to happen. If anything, Hogan's presence made it worse. He had a lot to lose if Cain was given back to the Eiloren clan. Cain knew him, and he was sure that Hogan wouldn't hesitate to attack the clan on his own to get Cain back if he had to.

What's going on? Cain asked.

Nothing bad. Well, not for you. Nothing that's about to be said changes your situation. I promise.

It should have helped, but it didn't. Something *had* happened, and it had to do with the Eiloren clan.

You're freaking him out, Morven said as he came closer. *It's good to see you, Cain. I'm sorry we had to ask you to come here the way we did, but it's important.*

I'm listening, Cain said.

We just had a visit from one of the Ogorth clan's spies. He was tasked with keeping an eye on the Eiloren clan, and he had news for us.

Cain was almost too afraid to ask. *They're going to attack?*

Morven shook his head. *They're not. But they've been talking with the queen's cousin, and I'm sure you know who I mean.*

Cain did. *Does this mean the queen is in trouble?* He could see her at the end of the room, still talking with Slavin and Octavia. Orran was there, too, and he looked angry, but he wasn't saying anything. Cain couldn't see the spy, but it would make sense he hadn't stuck around to meet him.

We don't know yet.

What's going to happen next, then? he asked.

The queen is waiting for her cousin. She's going to confront him and ask him about his contact with your old clan. We'll see what happens and make decisions based on his reaction and what he says.

They didn't have to wait long, but it felt like a lifetime. Hogan stuck close to Cain, something for which Cain was grateful, but that also flustered him. It reminded him of how much he had to lose if what happened next went wrong. He wasn't about to push Hogan away, though, and he leaned against him as they waited.

The queen was going to confront her cousin with only Morven and Orran by her side. That meant that Cain, Hogan, Slavin, and Octavia were still in the corner. There was no way the queen's cousin wouldn't see them, and Cain was worried about that, but Hogan reassured him that it was on purpose. Apparently, the queen wanted her cousin to see who he was hurting, and more importantly, that she had guards who wouldn't hesitate to intervene if she was in danger. The door opened, and the guard who had come to fetch Cain looked in. *Your Majesty? Your cousin is here.*

The queen was on her throne now, and she sat up

straighter. *Let him in.*

Cain had seen this dragon around the palace, but he'd steered away from him and the people with him. They didn't look like a friendly bunch, and Cain hadn't wanted to risk it. He was unsurprised to find out he'd been right but also nervous. He had no idea what was going to happen, and he wasn't looking forward to whatever it would be.

You wanted to talk to me? Caven drawled.

I did, the queen confirmed. *It has to do with your contact with the Eiloren clan.*

Cain held his breath, expecting Caven to be offended by the queen's words. Instead, he answered calmly, *I'm not sure what you're talking about.*

And I'm sure you are. I know you had contact with the Eiloren clan. I want to know what was said.

Nothing of importance. It's diplomacy, as I'm sure you're aware. I have contacts with many clans in the area. I would think you knew about it.

Cain was offended for the queen. She was good at her job, though, and if she felt the same, it didn't show in her expression. *I can give you the names of the people you talked to if it helps refresh your memory.* She did just that, and with every name, Cain's stomach churned harder. Those were all people close to the king who knew what the king wanted and who would do anything to give it to him.

Like I said, diplomacy, Caven answered. *Now, if you don't have anything else to ask, I have work to do. I'm sure you do, too.*

The queen looked like she wanted to tear Caven's head off his shoulders, and Cain would be happy to help if she tried. Instead, she nodded. *You can go. Keep away from the Eiloren clan, though. That includes any diplomatic relationship you have with them.*

I suppose I'll have to obey your order. Have a good day, cousin.

Cain watched him walk back to the doors, knowing this was nowhere near over.

Chapter Seven

Something was wrong. Hogan was sure of that, even though he had no idea what that something was. It no doubt had to do with the queen's cousin and the Eiloren clan.

When the queen had talked to her cousin a few weeks earlier, Hogan had to resist the urge to punch him in the face. He'd been disrespectful, just like always, but in this case, something crucial to Hogan was at stake. He needed to protect Cain, and if Caven wasn't going to help, Hogan wouldn't hesitate to hit him.

He hadn't. He wasn't sure how he'd found the strength, but he was glad he had. The problem was that they didn't have anything new. Right after the queen talked to her cousin, Cain had explained that the names she'd mentioned belonged to people close to the king. The Eiloren clan was planning something, and no one knew what. It meant that all of them were hyper-vigilant, waiting for that something to happen, and it wasn't good.

Hogan had snapped at Slavin three times today already. He'd also apologized three times, and Slavin had said it was okay, but it wasn't. Hogan didn't want to be angry at his friends. He wasn't, not really, but he couldn't help but think about what they were waiting for and what was going to happen if they couldn't find a way to keep Cain safe.

But it had been weeks, and *nothing* was happening. Hogan didn't know what that meant, but he did know that he wouldn't rest easy until he was sure Cain was safe, which was impossible for the moment. It made him want to hit something—possibly the queen's cousin or even the Eiloren king.

"You're worrying again," Cain said.

Hogan had been trying to hide it, but he'd clearly failed. "I just don't like waiting for something to happen." He looked at Cain, who was in the corner of their room putting his egg into the small nest they'd made for it.

Now that Hogan and Cain shared what had once been Hogan's nest, there was less space for the egg, and they were both afraid to roll on top of it while sleeping. So far, that was the only reason they had to move it while they were in the nest, but Hogan hoped that eventually, there would be more. He couldn't remember ever wanting anyone as much as he wanted Cain, but he also loved him, which was one of the reasons he was giving Cain time and space.

"I don't know how not to worry when it comes to you," Hogan continued. He was already in their nest waiting for Cain to come to bed. They were in their human form, which didn't feel as strange as it had initially.

Their little group of friends had tightened around Cain, keeping an eye on him but also spending more time with him. They were closer than ever, and since Sheldon and Blake had only one form, they all spent most of their time as humans. Hogan had to admit he didn't mind. It meant he could ignore most dragons because he couldn't hear them, and the ones he didn't want to ignore knew to shift and talk to him in their human form. This way, Hogan heard a lot less gossip and insults directed at Cain or any of their friends, which meant he'd only punched two dragons recently. Morven thought it was two dragons too many, but Hogan was satisfied.

Besides, Hogan loved kissing. He would never admit it to anyone, but he thought that was one of the best reasons for him and Cain to stay in their human form. He felt like he would never get enough of kissing Cain, which meant he had to get used to spending most of his time as a human. So far, he hadn't found any reason not to. He hoped that would continue.

Cain finally finished fussing over the egg. He got to his feet and moved toward the nest, apparently ready to go to bed. Hogan grabbed one of the blankets he'd set aside, and as soon as Cain was next to him, he covered both of them, making sure no inch of skin was uncovered. It wasn't cold exactly, but the palace could be chilly, and he never wanted Cain to be uncomfortable.

Cain sighed heavily and pressed his body against Hogan's. "I'm worried, too," he said.

"I don't want you to worry," Hogan murmured.

"How about I stop if you do?"

Hogan shook his head. There was no way he could stop worrying, not until he knew for sure that Cain would be okay. "I just *know* something is going to happen. I hate not knowing when or what, though."

"You can't worry yourself to death about this."

"You are. Why can't I do the same?"

Cain chuckled. "Fine. How about we agree that both of us will try our best not to obsess over this? Whatever the Eiloren clan is planning, it'll happen whether or not we worry about it. What we're doing is helping them and not us, and I don't want it to continue."

"We need to be ready when it happens," Hogan said. That was the only thing he could think about.

Cain patted Hogan's chest. "And we will be. I trust you and our friends. I know I'm safe and that nothing will happen to me."

Hogan wished he could be as sure as Cain. He supposed that was one of the big differences between them. "I trust them, too, but no one else. That's the problem."

Cain sighed and pressed himself closer. "I get it. But I'm

over this, Hogan. I don't want to spend the rest of my life worrying just in case the Eiloren clan decides to do something. I have other, more important things to focus on."

"Yeah? And what are those things?"

Cain smiled. It was a kind of smile that was reserved for Hogan and that always stole his breath away. When Cain smiled like this, Hogan could think of nothing but kissing him.

"My egg, of course," Cain said, apparently not knowing the effect he had on Hogan. "And you."

Hogan sucked in a breath. "Me?"

Cain rubbed his face against Hogan's chest. "Always. I couldn't imagine a life without you in it, and I don't want to." He sighed. "I know the situation is complicated, but I want us to focus on our future. I feel like we've barely had the time to be together since we found out the queen's cousin was talking to the Eiloren clan, and when we do, you're always looking over your shoulder. I'm not much better. I just want to focus on us as a couple."

"We can do that," Hogan said with a rough voice. He wasn't sure what Cain meant exactly, but he supposed he would find out soon enough. "We could go on a date? We shouldn't leave the palace, but we could organize something here in our rooms. I'm sure Sheldon and Morven would be happy to babysit the egg, and we could grab food and spend the evening together."

Cain didn't answer. Hogan frowned, wondering if his idea was so bad that Cain didn't know what to say, but when he looked down, Cain's eyes were closed and he was breathing steadily.

He was asleep.

Hogan smiled. Cain was often exhausted by the end of the day because he tried to do too much. He spent time with Blue because he liked the baby and because he wanted to know what to do when his child was born. He spent time with Sheldon, trying to reassure him about his and Morven's baby and helping him search through the old books of the library to see if they had records of dragon and human hybrids. He took care of the rooms he and Hogan lived in while Hogan was at work, and Hogan had found out that Cain also visited his parents, something he barely did himself.

Then of course, there was the worrying. It took a lot of energy, and even though Cain had just said he wanted to stop obsessing over the Eiloren clan and their plans, it wasn't easy to actually do it. Even though the Eiloren clan had never been a family to Cain, it had been his home since he was born, and it couldn't be easy to accept the fact that they'd never wanted what was best for him, but rather, what was best for the king.

Hogan held Cain closer and kissed his hair, inhaling the scent that had become so familiar to him. No matter how hard it was to focus on something that wasn't the Eiloren clan, he would try, and so would Cain. Because Cain was right—they couldn't and shouldn't put their lives on hold because of something that might never happen.

Cain woke up like he'd been waking up for the past few weeks—warm, wrapped in Hogan's arms, and horny. He'd always managed to hide it, but this morning, he couldn't remember why he should. He and Hogan were together. They were a couple, and couples had sex.

The last time he'd done it, he'd been in his dragon form, and he hadn't loved the dragon he was doing it with. He'd hoped that would change, but he hadn't really cared. He'd just wanted to have a baby, and he had.

Hogan was different. He and Cain loved each other, and even if one day that changed, Cain would never regret having loved Hogan and making love to him. He just had to be sure

Hogan wanted it as much as he did, which was hard, since Hogan was still asleep and Cain didn't want to be a creep by rubbing all over him.

Cain sucked in a breath and pulled his hips back. He wanted to roll out of the nest and go to the bathroom since it had worked so well before, but this time, Hogan didn't let him go. Instead of loosening, his hold on Cain tightened, and he pulled Cain closer. When he kissed Cain's temple, Cain realized he was awake.

"Where are you going?" Hogan asked in a rough voice.

"The bathroom. Did you need anything?"

"Just you."

Hogan buried his face against Cain's neck, causing Cain to suck in a breath. He didn't know what this meant about what Hogan wanted, and the best way to find out was to ask. Cain had to swallow a few times before he managed to get the words out. "What are you doing?" he murmured.

"I want you, Cain. I've wanted you since the first time I saw you, and I thought you were a disaster waiting to happen. That hasn't changed, but my feelings for you have. I love you. I know we never talked about being together physically, even though we're a couple, but if you're okay with it—"

Cain wiggled his way down until he and Hogan could look each other in the eyes. "I'm more than okay with it. I wasn't sure you would be, which is why I was going to the bathroom." He took a chance and pressed his hips forward. There was no way Hogan could ignore Cain's arousal.

Hogan stared at Cain for a moment. Cain waited, holding his breath. Whatever was about to happen wouldn't make or break their relationship, but it was still scary. Even though he and Hogan were together and in love, this was a pivotal change in their relationship. Things would never be the same after what was about to happen, one way or another.

Thankfully, Hogan didn't waste time. He kissed Cain, and

Cain melted against him, relieved and horny at the same time. He didn't know what he wanted, just that he wanted Hogan—to feel his skin against his, to kiss him and lose himself in making love. Everything else would come naturally.

Hogan rolled them until Cain was under him. He hovered there, looking down at Cain, their cocks pushing against each other as they breathed. Cain ached to feel Hogan inside of him, and since he'd had an egg recently, that was the safest way to do this. He and Hogan hadn't talked about when Hogan had last been fertile, and Cain didn't want to take the chance, not without talking to Hogan first.

He wrapped his legs around Hogan. Hogan shuddered and tried to move back, but Cain didn't want to let him go. "What do you want?" he asked.

"Anything. Everything. I don't know where to start, but I don't want to hurt you."

"You would never hurt me. There's no one I trust more in the world than you, Hogan. I want this, and I want you. Whatever you're ready to give me."

Hogan stared for a moment longer.

Cain knew enough of Hogan's past to be aware of the fact that he didn't trust easily, not even people he had relationships with. Cain was different, even though he didn't understand why or how. It didn't matter, anyway. What mattered was that Hogan loved him and wanted this with him, and that he trusted him.

Hogan leaned down and kissed Cain again. Cain could feel Hogan's hands moving on his skin, making him shiver in pleasure. He allowed Hogan to explore his body as he did the same with Hogan's.

Unlike Cain, Hogan was hard, with muscles everywhere. Cain could feel them flex under his fingertips, and it made him want to bury himself inside Hogan. Hogan's arms caged him, but instead of making him panicky, it made him feel safe.

Whatever happened next, he knew Hogan would make sure it was good for him, and that, more than anything, showed Cain how much he cared. Cain had made the right choice, even though falling in love with Hogan hadn't truly been one.

Hogan's fingertips brushed against the head of Cain's cock. Cain's body tensed in expectation. He let out a breath when Hogan stroked his fingers up and down his length. It wasn't nearly enough, but if that was all Hogan could give him, it would have to be.

It wasn't. Hogan had so much to give, more than most people realized. He kissed Cain as he continued touching him, his fingers moving alternatively on Cain's cock and into his pouch. He was driving Cain crazy, pushing him to the brink of pleasure only to move his hand away before Cain could come. It made Cain want to yell at him, but since he didn't want to ruin the mood, he decided to do some teasing himself.

He pushed Hogan, and even though he wouldn't have been able to move him in normal circumstances, this was anything but. With a few moves, Cain had Hogan on his back and was sitting on top of him. Both their pouches were wet, a sign that they were ready to take this to another level, but Cain was going to take his time.

He kissed down Hogan's chest, exploring every inch of skin he could get to. He was glad when Hogan didn't try to stop him, and he grinned when he felt Hogan shudder under him. It felt as if Hogan was trying hard not to reach for him. This was becoming torture for both of them, though, so Cain stopped once he reached Hogan's groin.

He hovered his lips just above the head of Hogan's cock, but instead of touching it, he moved back up. Hogan groaned, his hands reaching for Cain. He grabbed Cain's hips and pulled him up, and the head of his cock caught in Cain's pouch.

Hogan froze. He stared at Cain with wide eyes as if he

didn't know what to do. Cain did, and he grabbed Hogan's cock, holding it up for him to slide into his pouch. Once the head was in, he reclined against Hogan's chest, kissing him.

It was heaven. It was so very different from doing it in his dragon form, if anything, because he could kiss Hogan. He loved kissing Hogan, and he never had enough of it. He was pretty sure Hogan felt the same, but at the moment, it felt like Hogan couldn't kiss him back. He was panting, his mouth open as he stared at Cain while they moved.

That was fine with Cain. He kissed Hogan's cheeks, his nose, his eyebrows. He kissed every bit of Hogan's face he could reach, lingering on his lips even though Hogan wasn't kissing him back.

Until he was. Hogan's arms went around Cain, and he rolled them again. As soon as Cain was on his back, Hogan thrust into him. Cain yelped, surprised, then clung to Hogan as he continued moving. His cock was pressed between both their stomachs, and the friction was maddening. He tightened his muscles, grinning when Hogan moaned loudly. He might be stuck under Hogan, but that didn't mean he couldn't do anything.

"I love you," Hogan murmured. "Love you, love you."

Cain pushed himself up and kissed him. "I love you, too."

They didn't talk anymore after that. They were both chasing pleasure, and when Cain came, Hogan wasn't far behind. It was as if he'd waited for Cain to come, which didn't surprise Cain. Many people thought Hogan was an angry dragon, someone who was better alone than with people, but it was far from the truth. Hogan cared much more than a lot of people.

Once it was over, they stayed wrapped around each other in the nest. Cain's body felt boneless, but it was morning, and they were going to have to move soon.

Hogan groaned. "I don't want to go to work."

"You could stay home, but we both know you'd be angry at yourself for it."

"We also have to go to dinner with my parents tonight. Can I tell them we changed our minds?"

There was whining Hogan's voice. This was the side of him Cain only saw when his parents were involved.

"I like your parents. I want to spend time with them." And he knew Hogan would never take that away from him.

"Fine. I want you to know I'm not happy about it, though."

"I'll make sure not to forget that." Cain kissed Hogan's lips. "Now, you have to get up and go to work. The baby and I will be here when you come back."

They would be here for Hogan for the rest of Hogan's life if that was what Hogan wanted.

Hogan didn't want to do this. He'd avoided dinner at his parents' even before he'd met Cain, but he'd had better excuses then. Now that Cain was in his life, it was impossible to avoid them. They wanted to get to know Cain and spend time with him, and Cain wanted the same. There was no way Hogan could say no, not when he knew Cain needed a family.

So here he was, trudging behind Cain as they walked down the hallway toward his parents' rooms. Cain was holding the egg as he talked about what he'd done today, and Hogan found himself staring more often than not.

He was fascinated by Cain, but more importantly, he couldn't quite believe that Cain had chosen him. It didn't make sense, but he wasn't going to argue. He knew how lucky he was.

"You're quiet," Cain said.

Hogan arched a brow. "Aren't I always?"

"Not with me. What's going on in that head of yours?"

"I was just thinking about how lucky I am to have you in

my life." He caught Cain's waist and pulled him closer, kissing his cheek. As he did so, a dragon walked past them and made a sound Hogan didn't like. He leaned away from Cain and snarled, staring at the dragon until they were gone.

When he turned back to Cain, Cain was smiling. "You do realize you don't have to be that protective of me, right? That dragon didn't mean anything."

"How do you know? To me, it sounded like they had something against us kissing in the hallway."

"Or maybe they were just surprised to see you do something that isn't snarling and growling." Cain patted Hogan's arm. "But don't stop on my account. You know I like you growling."

If Hogan's skin had been lighter, Cain would have seen him blush. As it was, he didn't, and thankfully, they'd reached the rooms where Hogan had grown up. The door swung open before he even managed to knock, and his mother, Safira, stood there, in her human form, staring at them. She was beaming, just like always when she saw Cain and Hogan together, which made Hogan groan. "Hi, Mom," he said.

"Come in, come in. Your mother and father are in the kitchen."

Hogan's rooms were small compared to the ones his parents lived in, which made sense. He had what most dragons would think of as a bachelor pad, while this was a home for a family. The nest wasn't in the main room, instead set up in a bedroom at the back. There was also the room in which Hogan had grown up, while the main room held the kitchen, a table, and a few couches. It was still like it had been while Hogan was growing up, and coming back here always made him feel younger.

His parents were on Cain and the egg as soon as they noticed him. It was embarrassing, but Cain seemed to thrive on the attention. Hogan stood to the side, allowing his parents to fuss over Cain. Of course, his father noticed, and he moved aside, coming closer. "We're happy to see you," he said.

Hogan couldn't help but smile. "I can see that."

"I meant both you and Cain, but you know that. How are things going?"

"Same old, I suppose. What's for dinner? I'm hungry."

Hogan's father laughed and clapped his shoulder. "Why don't you come help me in the kitchen while your mothers and Cain talk?"

Hogan groaned, but he followed. As he helped his father, he couldn't help sneaking peeks at Cain. Since he'd arrived at the Ogorth clan, he'd been flourishing. It was never as obvious as what he was with Hogan's family, though.

Cain had never known his parents, and Hogan knew he'd yearned for them. He probably still did, but Hogan's family soothed something inside of him. They weren't his blood, but they were his family, and they loved him

That was why no matter how embarrassed Hogan was, he would always agree to visit them if that was what Cain wanted. Cain needed more than just him. He needed friends and family, and he had them now.

CHAPTER EIGHT

Cain examined his egg. The healer thought it was due to open any day now, and Cain couldn't wait. He kept catching himself staring at it, even though he knew it wouldn't change anything. The egg wouldn't open sooner if he watched it.

He doubted any parent would have been able to step away. Right now, he didn't have anything to do but watch his egg and worry about the future. If he let his thoughts drift, they always went to the Eiloren clan and what they would do eventually. Maybe they were waiting for the egg to open. It would be easier for them to steal the egg, though, so Cain wasn't convinced.

A knock on the door made him jump. It always did after that guard had come to fetch him for the queen. But nothing much had happened since then, and Cain had to admit he'd started to relax. Hogan was still tense, and he probably would be until they were sure the Eiloren clan wouldn't do anything. That made it hard for them to be a couple, but they were working through it, and Hogan was as protective and caring as always, maybe even more.

Late at night, when it was only the two of them in their rooms, he finally relaxed, and it made Cain happy. He understood that Hogan had always been protective of him and that it was his job, but it was so much more than that. Hogan loved him, and he wouldn't let anything happen to him.

Cain opened the door, smiling at Sheldon. "I didn't expect you."

Sheldon grinned. "You were staring at the egg, weren't you?"

Cain laughed. He and Sheldon had bonded a lot over having an egg. Sheldon might not have laid his and Morven's, but Morven was at work most days, while Sheldon was the one taking care of the egg. He and Cain had spent a lot of time together, and Cain enjoyed it. He'd been fascinated with humans, and he still was, even though he knew two of them now.

"Because you haven't been?" he asked instead of answering.

"Guilty as charged. Morven finds it hilarious, but I can see him doing the same. If he didn't have to go to work, he would be staring at it twenty-four seven."

"Well, I doubt anyone would blame him or you. Did you need anything?"

"Actually, I was about to offer for you to leave me your egg for a bit. I know you've been complaining about not having enough time with Hogan, and it's not going to get better once your egg hatches. Maybe you could take advantage of the time you still have?"

Cain was touched. "That would be great." He'd just been thinking that he and Hogan didn't have enough time together, and Sheldon wasn't wrong. Once they had the baby, it would be even harder for them to be together. They should spend as much time as a couple as they could before it happened.

"Morven and I were lucky that we had time together before he got pregnant. That hasn't been the case for you, and I know it's been worrying you."

Cain sighed. "Not worrying, exactly."

"But you've been thinking about it."

"It's a change from thinking about the Eiloren clan."

Sheldon grimaced. "I see. I can't say I know how you feel,

but I'm worried about them, too. We all are. So, you want me to do this?"

Cain stepped back into the room and went to grab his egg. He rubbed it a bit as he went back to Sheldon, then paused to kiss the top before he got to the door. He thought Sheldon hadn't noticed, but when he reached him, Sheldon was smiling softly.

"I do that, too," he confessed. "It's kind of strange, because humans don't have eggs. Once the baby is born, it's there, and you don't have to wait anymore."

"It'll be okay." Cain wanted to promise so much more, but he couldn't, because no one knew what would happen to Sheldon's baby.

"I hope so." Sheldon made grabby hands. "Now give me my nephew. Take some time off, pamper yourself, and have fun with Hogan. You can even leave the egg with me the entire night if you want, although I doubt you're going to."

"That might be a bit too much." Cain wasn't sure he could stay away from his baby for that long.

"Well, whatever you want, just let me know. Blake and I will spend some time with Blue. Then I'll go back to mine and Morven's rooms for the evening with both eggs."

"Thank you." Cain's mind was already trying to think up something he and Hogan could do.

When they were together, they tended to stick to Hogan's rooms, both because it was comfortable and because that way they didn't have to face anyone from the clan. Cain wouldn't say the clan hadn't welcomed him, but now that the news that the Eiloren clan wanted him back had spread, it was obvious that a few of them wished they could send him packing. Most didn't, but they still kept their distance, although that probably had more to do with Hogan than with anything else.

Cain didn't mind. He was fine with the group of friends he already had, and he understood where Hogan was coming from. It was hard to trust anyone new.

Once Sheldon had left with the egg, Cain closed the door and looked around. The rooms were a bit of a mess, but he had time to clean up. Hogan wasn't supposed to come back for at least another hour, possibly more, so maybe Cain could have a nice dinner ready for him when he arrived. He would have to go to the kitchen to see if there was anything cooked, since there was no kitchen in Hogan's rooms, but it would be worth it.

Cain and Hogan would probably have to move to bigger rooms once the baby was born, but Cain wasn't looking forward to it. He would miss this place.

He went to work picking up a few dirty dishes and stacking them on a table by the door, then taking out the blankets from the nest and shaking them out the window. He put them to wash, added more clean blankets to the nest, and kept the windows open for a bit.

When another knock came at the door, he smiled, sure it would be either one of their friends or one of Hogan's parents. They'd taken to coming around even when Hogan was at work, and Cain couldn't have been more pleased.

He swung the door open, freezing when he didn't recognize the dragon on the other side of it. He opened his mouth to ask what was going on, but the dragon pushed him into rooms and followed him inside, slamming the door behind them. The dragon was in their human form, but Cain couldn't say whether it was a male or female, although he suspected a male from the short hair and muscles.

"What do you think you're doing?" Cain asked. "Leave these rooms. You don't belong here."

"Where's the egg?" The dragon looked around.

Cain's knees almost buckled at the relief that the egg was safe. "Who are you? What do you want?"

The dragon took a step closer. Cain swallowed, knowing

this wasn't going to end well. "Where is the egg?" the dragon repeated.

"Not here. I'll make sure Morven knows about this. He won't be happy about the way you barged in and made demands."

The dragon snorted. "As if I care. Where did you put it if it's not here?"

"With the queen's son."

The dragon swore. "Well, I suppose you'll be better than nothing."

Cain took a step back. He eyed the front door, wondering if he could get to it before the dragon caught him. He started moving, but the dragon was faster. He grabbed Cain's arm and pulled him forward, shaking him. "Where do you think you're going?"

"Let me go!" Cain yelled, hoping someone would notice what was going on.

The dragon twisted him until they were facing each other, then hit him. The taste of blood invaded Cain's mouth as he stumbled back, one hand to his face. The other was still in the dragon's grasp.

Cain tried to pull, but the dragon raised his hand again. "Don't," Cain begged.

The dragon didn't stop. His hand came down, hitting Cain again, and this time, the dragon let him go. The force of the punch pushed him back, and he landed against the wall. The back of his head hit the hard surface, making him see stars.

The world tilted around him, and he could feel himself slip away. His head hurt, and he tried to fight it, but he couldn't.

Everything turned black.

Hogan glared at a dragon crossing his path in the hallway. He didn't have a reason to, but Cain always protested when he did something like this, and he felt the need to let everyone know that even though he was in a relationship now, he was still the same Hogan he'd always been.

Growling and snarling, just like Cain liked him.

He grinned when the dragon rushed away with barely a glance back. He might be a family man now, but he still had it.

"That was something," Slavin drawled.

Hogan glared at him. "Don't you have something better to do than following me around?"

"I'm not following you. We just happen to be walking the same way."

"Bullshit. Your rooms are two hallways down."

"It's a shortcut."

Hogan narrowed his eyes. "You want to see Cain, don't you?"

Slavin laughed and raised his hands. "All right. I do, but don't start thinking stupid things. I'm not in love with him or anything like that. I just like him and want to see him. Surely, you can understand that."

Hogan could, and he trusted his friend and the man he loved. Still, he playfully growled at Slavin, making him jump away. When Slavin did, Hogan laughed, ignoring Slavin's glare.

"That wasn't funny," Slavin complained.

"It was for me. And you know I don't care if you spend time with Cain. You wouldn't be the only one. I'm pretty sure Blake and Sheldon have seen Cain more often than I did this week."

Slavin grimaced. "Eventually, something is going to give, and you'll be able to spend all of your time with him again."

"I know. But keeping him safe is more important than spending time together." Even though Hogan missed Cain like crazy. They saw each other every day and shared a nest, but he wanted so much more. Like Slavin had said, he *would* get that more eventually. He just had to make sure the Eiloren can wouldn't come after Cain first.

They reached Hogan's door, and he quickly knocked before opening the door.

"You knock on your own door?" Slavin asked.

"I just want Cain to know I'm here in case he's busy."

"Seeing you so in love is kind of scary," Slavin said as he followed Hogan inside.

Hogan didn't answer. He couldn't do anything but stare at the disaster of a room in front of him.

"What happened here?" Slavin murmured.

"I don't know."

The room was a mess. It was obvious someone had been looking for something, and Hogan could too easily imagine what it had been. The couch was upside down, its pillows ripped and their insides spread all over the room. The nest wasn't a nest anymore, having been torn apart, and the blankets were thrown around. There wasn't one surface free of mess, and bile rose in Hogan's throat.

"Cain?" he called out.

He wasn't surprised when he didn't get an answer. "Check the bathroom. I'm calling Morven," Slavin said.

Hogan was relieved he wasn't alone. He moved toward the bathroom, but before he could reach it, the smell hit his nose. He would recognize the scent of blood anywhere, but especially so if it was Cain's. He had bled a bit when he'd laid his egg, and that moment was seared in Hogan's mind. Something had happened to Cain, and he needed to find out what and where Cain was.

He followed the trail of blood, ignoring Slavin, who was on the phone. When Hogan walked out, the door opened, and Slavin noticed and rushed after him.

"What are you doing?"

Hogan didn't have time to answer. Instead he shifted, since his sense of smell would be better in his dragon form. As soon as he was done, he followed it down the hallway. He couldn't think of anything that wasn't finding Cain and making whoever had hurt him pay. He wasn't sure where he was going, and it didn't matter. He *would* find Cain.

Something heavy landed on his back, flattening him to the floor. He roared so loud he was pretty sure he felt the walls vibrate. Whatever was on his back didn't move, though, and he tried twisting around, snapping his teeth.

You have to calm down.

Hogan stopped moving at the sound of Slavin's voice in his head. *What are you doing?*

Trying to stop you from doing something stupid. Morven said to wait for him.

Hogan tried to buck Slavin off, but he wasn't moving. *I don't care what Morven said. I have to get to Cain.*

I get that. I promise you'll find him, but you're going to do something stupid if you don't think. You're not thinking right now, Hogan, and you're dangerous. Cain wouldn't want you to hurt yourself or anyone who didn't have something to do with this.

Hogan took a deep breath. Slavin was right, and they both knew it. Freaking out and panicking wasn't going to help Cain, and that was Hogan's main goal.

"What's going on?" someone asked.

Hogan growled at them without looking. He didn't expect the slap on his nose, and he reeled back as Slavin rolled off him. He blinked at Octavia, who was staring down at him, her hands on her hips.

She pointed her index finger at his nose. "Don't you dare growl at me."

Slavin and Hogan both shifted back. Slavin quickly explained what was going on, and just as he finished, Morven and Orran arrived, too. Hogan was touched that everyone seemed to want to help, but they weren't moving fast enough.

"Tell me what happened," Morven ordered using his serious voice.

Hogan found himself obeying. "Slavin and I went to my rooms. We'd just left work, and he wanted to have a chat with Cain. When we arrived, Cain was nowhere to be seen, and the room was a mess. I smelled his blood." Hogan had to swallow. His mouth was dry, which didn't make it easy.

"The egg?" Octavia asked.

"It's with Sheldon," Morven answered.

Hogan could have kissed him. His main objective had been to find Cain, but he'd been terrified for the egg, too. Even though he now knew the egg was safe, he needed to see it and make sure for himself that everything was okay.

Morven's expression softened. "Why don't we head to my rooms? I already sent someone to tell the queen something was happening, but I'd rather not involve more people than need to be involved. I think our little group should be enough to get Cain back, although I'll make sure to have a team back us up, just in case. I'm sure Hogan needs to see the egg, and that would be better done in a place we know is safe."

Hogan nodded. The only thing he could think of was Cain and making sure he was fine, but he could do nothing about that for now. What he *could* do was protect Cain's baby, and that was what Cain would want him to do. No matter how much he wanted to head out and find the man he loved, he wouldn't be able to do anything on his own, and he had responsibilities.

Cain would kick his ass if he didn't take care of their egg.

As they walked down the hallways, Hogan could hear both Morven and Orran on the phone, talking urgently. He had no idea what they were doing, and he couldn't focus. Even though he had experience in this kind of thing, it was as if his mind wasn't working. The only things he could think about were Cain and the egg, and the same thoughts went round and round in his mind.

He'd promised to keep both of them safe, and he'd failed.

When Cain woke up, he was sure his head was going to explode. It had never hurt so badly, and it was all he could do not to moan. He almost did, but he remembered what had happened to cause him the headache, and he knew he couldn't afford to draw attention.

So he kept both his eyes and his mouth shut, and he listened.

He didn't know where he was, but the ground under him was cold and hard. He wiggled his fingers, almost grimacing at the pinprick of pain in his wrists. He was tied up at the wrists and ankles, but thankfully, his hands were tied in the front. He touched the ground under him, feeling earth and hard bits and pieces.

He wasn't in the palace anymore, then.

He hadn't expected to be, not after what had happened. He'd been kidnapped, and he almost sobbed at the thought of what would have happened if Sheldon hadn't picked up his egg a mere ten minutes before the dragon had invaded his rooms. Whoever that dragon was, he was obviously working for the Eiloren clan, which meant they wanted both Cain and the egg.

"Do I have to do everything myself?" a voice snarled.

"It's not my fault the egg wasn't in the rooms," someone answered. Cain was pretty sure it was the dragon who had kidnapped him.

"It was supposed to be. You just had to do your job. I promise that this wasn't my fault," the first dragon added. Cain thought he recognized the voice, but he wasn't a hundred percent sure.

"We don't care about promises," a third dragon said, and

this voice, Cain recognized.

His stomach dropped. It was Juno, the Eiloren's king right-hand woman. She was here to take Cain and his egg back to the Eiloren clan, just like Cain had suspected would eventually happen.

"We can get the egg," the first dragon said.

Cain carefully opened one eye to see who was talking. He was only half surprised to see Caven, the queen's cousin. They'd known he was talking with the Eiloren clan, but Cain hadn't expected him to betray the queen the way he had.

"And if you do and hand it over to us, we'll keep our side of the deal. In the meantime, though, we have nothing to give you."

"You promised you would help me." Caven sounded angry.

"And you promised you would deliver both the dragon and the egg. I only see one of those here, which means you didn't fulfill your side of the deal. We won't, either, until you do. That's all I have to say about it."

"It's not my fault the egg wasn't with its father!"

"Don't make me repeat myself," Juno snapped. "I don't care what's your fault and what isn't. We had a deal, and since you didn't bring us what was included in that deal, the king won't help you take your cousin's place on the throne. Call us again once you have everything we demanded."

"What am I supposed to do with him in the meantime?" Caven asked. He pointed a finger at Cain, and Cain slammed his eyes shut.

He couldn't breathe. He'd known the Eiloren clan was behind this, but he hadn't thought Caven would go to these lengths to get the throne. He'd betrayed the Ogorth clan, and if anyone found out, he would be in trouble. That wouldn't matter if he got what he wanted from the Eiloren clan, but he wouldn't, because Sheldon and the others would have noticed Cain was gone by now, and they'd keep the egg safe.

A roar made Cain jerk. He opened his eyes to see Caven had shifted and was reaching for a young tree. He grabbed it and tore it out of the ground, then threw it toward Cain, who only had a few seconds to try to scramble out of the way, which was impossible with his hands and ankles bound. The tree hit him, knocking the breath out of him. He was dazed for a few seconds, but he could still hear Caven rage nearby. The tree might have hurt Cain, but it also covered and hid him, which made him feel safer, albeit barely. A tree wouldn't do much if Caven attacked him in his dragon form, but maybe being out of sight would make Caven forget he was there.

Eventually, though, someone would remember Cain. He didn't know what would happen to him when they did, but he could imagine. Apparently, Juno wouldn't take him back without the egg, which left him in Caven's hands. If Caven couldn't retrieve the egg—and Cain knew he wouldn't be able to, because Hogan would tear his head off if he as much as tried—he wouldn't need Cain anymore. The Eiloren clan wouldn't help him unless he had both Cain and the egg, but it wouldn't make sense for him to keep Cain once he knew there was no way he was putting his hands on the egg.

Cain would die. He'd made his peace with death when he'd escaped the Eiloren clan. He'd hoped he would manage to lay his egg and live in the forest with his baby, but he'd suspected it would be much harder than that. He'd believed he would die eventually. When he'd met Hogan, though, he'd forgotten about death. He was safe, and he had a new life.

Would he survive long enough to live it? It wouldn't make sense for Caven to keep him around, not when Cain was one of the few who knew what he was trying to do and wasn't useful anymore. Cain wished he had a way to let the queen know what was happening, although she probably suspected. More importantly, Cain wished he could contact Hogan and tell him how much he loved him.

He knew Hogan would raise his baby. He would be a perfect father, which was all Cain could hope for.

Something else crashed nearby. Cain curled into as tight a ball as he could, hoping that this way nothing would land on him. He almost shifted, but he didn't know for sure what he'd been tied up with, and he didn't want to risk the material being something that might shift with him, or worse, that would stay as it was and hurt him even more.

Instead, he waited for the end he was sure was coming.

As soon as Hogan was in Morven and Sheldon's rooms, he rushed toward the egg. Sheldon had brought back both Cain's egg and his to his rooms, just in case. The entire palace was on alert by now, everyone looking for Cain, but Hogan knew they wouldn't find him. Whoever had him, it wouldn't have been smart for them to keep Cain close by. It was much better to take him out, and they'd probably had enough time to make that happen.

Hogan grabbed the egg and cradled it to his chest. He took a moment to check its surface, breathing easier once he saw it was intact. Not that he expected Sheldon to allow anything to happen to it, but he needed to be sure. Once he was, he turned to the rest of their group. All of them were gathered. They were talking, their expressions grim, and Hogan had to take a deep breath before he could join them.

"What's being done?" Sheldon asked.

"I have the guards going through the palace. They're supposed to visit every room to make sure Cain isn't there," Morven answered.

"What about the cameras? I should have thought to check them. It's my job." Sheldon's voice sounded tortured, as if he blamed himself for what happened.

Hogan didn't want him to feel that way. It was no one's fault but the person who had taken Cain, but before he could say anything, Sheldon already had his phone out. He was typing on the screen, his fingers flying. Hogan had no idea what he was doing, but he could imagine. Sheldon wanted Cain to be found, and he had access to all the cameras in the palace.

"Here," Sheldon said after a few moments. "I brought up the cameras from the hallway outside Cain and Hogan's rooms."

Everyone squeezed around him to be able to see the small screen. Hogan watched as Sheldon came around, knocked on the door, and had a quick conversation with Cain. He saw Cain hand over the egg, and he squeezed it harder to his chest. They had come so close to losing the egg, too, and he knew Cain would have never forgiven himself if something had happened to his baby. He'd done everything he could to save his child from the Eiloren clan and the future the baby would have had with them, yet they'd been so close to getting their hands on it anyway. The only reason they hadn't was that Sheldon had decided Hogan and Cain should spend some time on their own.

Once Sheldon left with the egg, Cain closed the door again, then nothing happened for about ten minutes. Sheldon fast-forwarded until another dragon appeared in front of the door. Hogan held his breath. The dragon knocked, and Cain opened the door. The dragon pushed him inside, and they both disappeared from view. Another five minutes, and the door opened. The dragon, now in their dragon form, walked out. They were holding something to their chest, but it wasn't possible to see what it was from a distance. Hogan knew, though.

"They took Cain," he said.

"And I recognize that man," Morven added. "Isn't that the brother of the dragon we had to send away?"

"You mean the one who attacked us?" Blake asked. "The one who was friends with the queen's cousin?"

The only reason Hogan didn't punch the wall was that he was still holding the egg. He should have known Caven had something to do with this. They'd been expecting him to act since they'd found out he had contact with the Eiloren clan. Now, he had, and Hogan was going to strangle him if he ever got his hands on him. He didn't care that Caven was royalty. He just wanted him to die.

Morven leaned closer. "I think so."

"Who cares who the dragon is?" Hogan snapped. "I only care about getting Cain back, and that's not going to happen if we stay here."

"We could try finding this dragon," Blake said.

"He won't be here anymore. If he truly works for Caven, both he and Caven would have left with Cain. You can try looking for them in the palace, but I guarantee you, they're not close by."

"I can bring up the cameras for all the exits," Sheldon intervened.

Hogan was grateful. He didn't want to yell at anyone, least of all one of his friends. He also didn't want to hurt Blake, but he was freaking out, and he hoped Blake would remember that.

A phone chirped, and everyone looked at theirs. Hogan didn't often have his with him because he had nowhere to put it when he was in his dragon form, but he knew Morven had a special pouch that he hung around his neck when he shifted. He kept his focus on his friend, knowing that if anyone could find out what was going on, it was him.

Sure enough, Morven nodded at whatever he was reading on the screen. "Lysander texted me. He thinks he knows where Cain was taken. He sent me the coordinates. I suppose everyone here who can is coming along?" Hogan was the first to nod, and Morven's gaze stopped on him. "I didn't mean you. You should stay here."

Hogan glared. "You can try to stop me, but I guarantee it won't go well. I'm not staying back."

"You don't have only yourself to think of now. You're the only parent the egg has left until we get Cain back. Do you really want to leave it alone?"

"We'll take care of it," Sheldon said. Morven glared at him, but Sheldon shook his head. "You can't think he's going to stay back. Would you if I was taken? Don't bother saying you would, because we both know it would be a lie. You'd give our egg to my brother, and you'd be the first in line trying to find me."

"Fine," Morven grumbled. He turned to Hogan. "You can come. I understand."

"I'm taking the egg with me." Hogan hadn't thought about the words before saying them, but he wasn't going back on them.

He could easily imagine what condition Cain would be in. When they found him, he'd need to see his baby, and he would freak out until he did. The least Hogan could do was take his egg to him and reunite them as soon as possible.

"You can't do that," Morven said. "It's dangerous."

"I'll keep the egg safe. It's my priority, along with Cain. I swear I'll stay out of any fighting that happens. I just want to find Cain and give him his egg back." It wasn't easy to put himself out of the fighting. Usually, Hogan was the first in there, punching and biting. This time, he would have to stay back, but he would be happy to do it if it meant Cain and the egg were safe.

Morven stared at him for a moment. Hogan expected him to say no and maybe try to convince him to stay after all, but thankfully, Morven nodded. "Fine. I'm not happy about this, but I get it. You can come, and you can bring the egg. Make sure you stay behind all of us, though. I don't want anything to happen to the egg or Cain."

They left Sheldon and Blake behind. Obviously, the two humans wished they could do more, and Hogan felt he had never understood them better than he did now. It was torture to be left behind when someone they loved was in danger, but there was nothing they could do. Their presence would be a hindrance, and they were aware of that. That was probably why they didn't protest and try to come along.

Hogan couldn't remember why he'd been wary of the brothers. They were good people, some of the best he'd ever known. The fact that they were humans didn't change that, and he would make sure they knew what he thought as soon as he and Cain were back.

First, though, he had to focus on what was about to happen. He'd made a lot of promises—to Cain that he would keep the egg safe in any circumstance, to Morven that he would stay back and not try to fight, to the queen that he would keep the clan safe. *That* was what he had to focus on, especially the promise he'd made to Cain.

In only a few hours, the three of them would be reunited, and Cain would be safe again. Hogan wouldn't contemplate any other outcome.

Once Caven's rage was over, Cain peeked between the branches of the tree still covering him. The forest was almost entirely silent around him, and it freaked him out more than the throwing around of trees. At least when Caven was angry, he wasn't focusing on Cain. Now that he was done throwing his tantrum, there was nothing else for him to focus on.

Cain couldn't see much from his position, but from the looks of it, the Eiloren clan people were gone. He couldn't see Juno, and he was grateful for that. She'd always scared him, and that hadn't changed since he'd run away.

"Where is he?" Caven bellowed.

Cain cringed, but there was nowhere for him to go. He had to wait under the tree for it to be pulled away, and when they did, he looked around, hoping for someone to save him. There was no one there, though, except for Caven and the dragon who had taken Cain. That dragon was still dragging the tree away, leaving Cain and Caven staring at each other.

"This is all your fault," Caven spat out.

He took a step forward, and Cain barely had the time to steel himself when he noticed Caven shifting his position. The kick to his legs wasn't a surprise, but it still hurt, and Cain tried to bundle himself into a ball to protect his face and stomach. That didn't stop Caven, unfortunately. He kept kicking Cain, swearing at him and insulting him.

He was panting by the time he was done. Cain had already been in pain, but now, it was even worse. It wasn't just his head and face anymore. It was also his legs, his back, his arms. His entire body felt sore and painful, and he just wanted to close his eyes and forget about everything.

Caven stood there, glaring down at him. He pointed a finger at Cain's face. "I could have had everything. Where did you put your egg?"

He would find out as soon as he went back to the palace, no doubt, but that didn't mean Cain would tell him. "Where it's safe," he murmured.

Caven growled and kicked Cain again. Cain whimpered, but thankfully, it was only one last kick. Once that was over, Caven stepped away. His cheeks were flushed, and his hair was all over the place. He didn't look like the queen's cousin anymore. He looked angry, as if he was ready to do anything to get his revenge.

"Kill him," he snapped.

Cain turned to look at the other dragon with wide eyes.

They were hovering there, staring from Caven to Cain. "We can't kill him. We need him for your plan."

"We don't. Didn't you hear that woman? She wanted the egg and him, and since we don't have both, she won't help."

"But if we find the egg—"

"Don't be an idiot. We won't find it, because by now, everyone will have realized he's gone. They'll keep an eye on the egg, and we won't be allowed anywhere near it. We don't need him anymore, which is why you have to kill him. If we take him back, he's going to talk. Do you want the queen to know what you did?"

The dragon snapped their mouth shut and shook their head. "No," they whispered.

"That's what I thought. Kill him and be done with it. I'm headed back to the palace. I expect this to be over by the time you get there, too." He paused and grinned. "Actually, maybe I'll stick around and watch you kill him. It's his fault I won't get the help I was promised. I wouldn't mind watching him die."

Cain swallowed. He pulled on his arms, even though it hurt, but the ties around his wrists didn't budge. He couldn't do anything as he watched the dragon who'd kidnapped him come closer.

The dragon crouched next to him and reached for him. Cain cringed.

He screwed his eyes shut, not wanting to watch death come for him. He felt a tugging on his wrists, then on his ankles.

Nothing else happened.

"What the fuck are you doing?" Caven asked. "I don't have time to waste. Hurry up."

Cain opened his eyes. The dragon was hovering above him, looking torn. They looked from Cain to Caven, who had stepped away but was still staring at them. When they turned back to Cain, Cain held his breath.

"You need to run," the dragon whispered.

When Cain looked down, he saw that the dragon had cut the ties. His ankles and hands were free, which meant he could run away.

Where would he go, though? They were in the forest, and he barely knew Ogorth clan territory. He didn't know where to go from here or even in what direction the palace was. He supposed he could shift and fly, and he'd get there soon enough, but he had no doubt that Caven would try to get to him. Cain had never been a strong flyer, and it was risky. It was better than lying here and waiting for someone to kill him, though.

He nodded curtly, then moved into a better position so he would be able to scramble away as soon as he had the opportunity. The dragon got to his feet and turned to Caven, blocking Cain's sight.

"What are you doing?" Caven asked. "I asked you to kill him."

"How should I do it?" the dragon asked.

Caven huffed. "I don't care, as long as he ends up dead."

Cain sprang to his feet and ran without looking back. He stumbled more times than he wanted, but his legs were on fire already from the kicks, and he thought it was a small miracle that he was even on his feet. He could hear Caven yell behind him and the other dragon answering, then someone scrambling to come after him.

He still ran. He couldn't afford to look back, no matter what was happening. His only chance was getting as far away as possible and waiting for Caven and the dragon to leave. He wasn't even sure he'd be able to shift, not with how painful everything was. He was going to try, though. He had to.

A loud noise coming from above him made him whimper. There was a crash, and trees fell, revealing a black dragon had landed there and was now facing him.

Cain didn't stop. He continued running, turning to the side instead of forward. He tried to shift, but he couldn't do it while he was running, and he couldn't afford to stop. He could barely even think, which would be a problem soon. He'd hoped that Caven and the other dragon would leave eventually, but maybe they wouldn't. They clearly had people supporting them, which pointed to the fact that Caven wasn't as stupid as Cain had thought. Cain wouldn't be able to do anything if he was confronted with dragons who were used to fighting. He was weak, so his only way out was running.

The dragon who had landed in the trees made a strange sound, and Cain heard him take to the air again. He hoped it meant the dragon had lost interest in him, but he knew better. Sure enough, a shadow passed above him, then the dragon landed in front of him again, knocking more trees to the ground.

Cain wasn't going anywhere, was he? This was it. He was going to die, and there was nothing he could do about it.

He stopped running and tried to stand tall. He was out of breath, struggling to get enough oxygen in his lungs. His face hurt and he was pretty sure it was swollen, while his legs felt like jelly and were no doubt already full of bruises. He wished his body wasn't injured this way because he didn't want Hogan to be hurt when they finally found him. There was nothing he could do, though, so he stood there, facing the dragon and praying his death would be quick.

Hogan had scared Cain, which was the last thing he'd wanted to do. He shifted as soon as his paws were on the ground, holding the egg to his chest now that the harness was too big.

Cain stood there, staring at him. His swollen face made it

obvious that he'd been beaten, and Hogan had to resist the urge to turn around and find Caven and whoever had helped him do this. They'd dared to touch Cain, hurt him, and Hogan wanted his revenge.

He remembered the promise he'd made to Morven. His only focus had to be on Cain and the egg, not on fighting and getting revenge. It was hard, but when he looked at Cain, he knew Morven was right. Cain needed him more than he needed to kick ass.

Cain made a strangled sound and threw himself forward. Hogan managed to catch him with his free hand, even though they both stumbled backward. Luckily, there was a tree there, and it held both of them up as Cain tried to bury himself against Hogan's chest and cried. It wasn't easy because the egg was between them, but Cain didn't seem to care. He pressed himself in the space between the egg and Hogan's arm, and Hogan wrapped his arm around him, needing to keep him close.

"I thought I was going to die," Cain said on a sob.

Hogan didn't know what to do. He didn't know how to comfort people, how to make sure they were okay. The only thing he was good at was fighting, and he couldn't do that in this situation. He was lost, right when he needed to know what to do the most. Cain needed him, but he didn't know how to be there for him.

"You won't," he promised. "Morven and the others probably caught up to Caven and whoever is helping him. They'll kick their asses, and they'll never be able to lay a hand on you again. Morven will make sure of it, and I will, too. I'm sorry I wasn't there for you. I should have been."

Cain looked up and shook his head. Hogan wanted to rage when he looked at him, but instead of doing that, he focused on what Cain was saying. "You can't stay with me twenty-four seven. You did everything you could, and it's not your fault I was taken."

"We knew something was going to happen, yet we didn't do anything to stop it."

"What could we have done? We didn't even know Caven was working with the Eiloren clan because they promised to help him take the throne. I just found out now."

They hadn't known for sure, but they'd suspected Caven's contact to be more than limited to normal diplomacy. If Hogan ever got his hands on Caven, he'd make sure the dragon never had a chance to come close to the throne, let alone sit on it.

"We should go back to the palace," Hogan said. He could hear the sound of people fighting somewhere in the forest, and he yearned to join them. It was much easier not to than he'd expected, though, especially when he focused on Cain.

Cain needed a healer, and he needed them as soon as possible.

Cain looked back to where to fighting was happening. "We should help them."

"You need to focus on yourself. There are more than enough of them to take on a few dragons, don't worry."

"The Eiloren clan is gone. There was only Caven and another dragon left a few minutes ago."

"See? Two dragons won't be a problem for Morven and the others. I promise."

Cain didn't look convinced, but he nodded. Just as he stepped away from Hogan, Hogan felt the egg vibrate against his chest. He looked down, his eyes widening at the sight of a crack running down its length.

"I swear I was careful," he hurried to say. "I never dropped it, and I had it in the harness the entire time."

Cain put a hand on Hogan's arm. "You didn't do anything. It's time."

Hogan's mouth went dry. "You mean the baby is coming

out?"

"The healer said it was bound to happen any day now. It looks like the baby chose today to meet us."

Hogan panicked. Why did he and Cain always have to do this alone in the forest? "We should fly back to the palace. We need a healer to be there when the egg hatches."

"I don't think we have time."

When Hogan looked down again, he understood what Cain was saying. There was another crack in the egg. In the place where the cracks crossed, a piece of shell was already peeling away. Hogan could see something pushing at it from inside the egg, and he knew Cain was right. They didn't have time to move. They had to do this here, and they had to do it now, because the baby wasn't going to wait.

"We should be doing this with people who know what they're doing," Hogan said.

"Maybe, but I don't think it matters."

"The baby should have all the best things and people in the world. Instead, look at us. You're hurting and need a healer, and this isn't the moment or place for the egg to hatch."

"But we don't have a choice. And besides, the baby is with the people who matter to him most."

Hogan blinked. "His father?" That had to be it.

Cain smiled. It looked painful, but that didn't stop him. "*Both* his fathers. His parents are here to help him, and that's what we're going to do."

He stepped away from Hogan and sat on the ground. He moved stiffly, which made Hogan want to drop the egg into his hands and go find Caven again, but Cain was right.

The baby wasn't waiting, and they needed both their parents there.

Hogan swallowed and sat next to Cain. He put the egg between them, and they both touched the surface as it continued cracking. Hogan didn't know a lot about egg hatching, but he did know that he should let the baby do this on their own as much as possible. He and Cain could help a bit, but not too much.

So they both watched the egg. It continued to vibrate and crack, and when the first piece of shell dropped to the ground, Hogan held his breath. An eye appeared at the opening, blinking and a bit cloudy. Hogan didn't know what to expect, but the eye didn't move, and he knew the baby was staring at him.

It wasn't fair. They should be staring at Cain, not at Hogan, so Hogan tried to twist the egg around to make that happen. Cain grabbed his wrist and shook his head, though.

"Don't."

"Why not? You laid this egg. It would only make sense for the baby to look at you instead of me."

"I'll tell you as many times as I need to, Hogan. You're the baby's other father. You have as much right as me to be here and watch this happening, and for the baby to look at you. I'm not jealous. If anything, I'm happier than I ever thought I could be, and it's mostly thanks to you. Let them do this the way they want to."

Hogan nodded, unable to say anything. When he looked at the egg again, the baby was still staring at him, and they clearly weren't happy. They were trying to push at the shell with their nose, then huffing in frustration when nothing happened.

"You think we should help?" Hogan asked.

"Why not? This is far from being a normal situation. I don't want to have to stay in the forest longer than strictly necessary."

Hogan waited for Cain to move. When he didn't, he reached for the egg. He wasn't going to ask again if Cain was sure Hogan should be the one doing this. He'd already told Hogan what he thought about it, and he knew what he was doing.

Hogan gently took hold of part of the shell and pulled. It was stronger than he'd expected, and he could understand the baby's frustration. *He* wasn't a baby, though, and with just a little more force, the top part of the egg cracked. The baby chippered and pushed again, and this time, the entire top part of the shell fell to the ground. It exposed the baby, and Hogan stopped breathing.

Just like the egg, the baby was a pale yellow. He wasn't like Cain, though. It was obvious his other father was a dark color, maybe purple, maybe blue. It wasn't obvious, but it made the baby a bit darker than Cain. When they moved, the darker color became more obvious as the light shone on their scales.

The baby looked like Hogan could truly be their other father.

Hogan couldn't breathe. He reached for the baby slowly, not wanting to scare them. He held out a finger, beaming when the baby sniffed it, then rubbed the side of their face against it. He jerked when he felt tiny teeth tug at his skin.

Cain laughed. "See? They already love you."

That got the baby's attention, and they turned to Cain. The baby had been fascinated by Hogan, but still in the egg. When they saw Cain, though, they tried to scramble out and almost fell in their haste to get to him. Hogan steadied the egg, and before he could do anything to help, the baby was out and climbing Cain's body.

Cain welcomed them with open arms. He cradled the baby to his chest, the beaming smile on his face almost enough to make Hogan forget how beaten up he was. "Welcome," he murmured. "I've been waiting for you."

And Hogan realized that he'd been waiting both for Cain and the baby all his life.

Chapter Nine

Cain was exhausted and sore, but he couldn't have been happier. He realized how strange it was to think that way, but he truly did. He might have been beaten up and looked death in the face, but he had Hogan, and they had their baby. There was nothing else Cain wanted or needed.

Going back to the palace had been an experience. Cain had tried to shift, but it hurt too much, and he hadn't been able to. That hadn't stopped Hogan. He'd shifted and stared at Cain until Cain finally climbed onto his back. It was strange, because Cain had never needed to do this and he'd never thought about carrying anyone while he was in his dragon form, but it wasn't as bad as he'd expected. Besides, Hogan would have kicked his ass if he hadn't agreed to it.

Cain held the baby against his chest as Hogan flew. He needed a bath, his bed, and possibly food, but most of all, he needed to be in his and Hogan's room and to have time for them to fit together as a family. He'd been kidnapped on the worst possible day, although he couldn't help but wonder if the baby had hatched today of all days on purpose. Maybe they'd sensed that Cain needed them. Maybe they'd wanted to be there.

Or maybe they were a baby and didn't understand that something had happened. The healer had told Cain the baby would come any day, and she hadn't been wrong.

Cain was relieved when Hogan finally landed. He was even more relieved when Morven, Octavia, Slavin, and Orran rushed toward them. He hadn't realized they were already done fighting Caven and the other dragon and that they were back at the palace. He'd barely thought about them over the past hour, but he doubted they would berate him for that.

Morven's eyes widened when he saw what Cain was carrying, and he helped him off Hogan's back. Hogan shifted as soon as Cain had stepped away, and he rushed toward him and the baby, wrapping an arm around Cain's shoulders and pulling him close.

"What the hell happened?" Morven asked, his gaze on the baby.

"Something we didn't expect," Hogan answered. He looked at Cain. "I talked to the baby."

Cain held his breath. He and Hogan had talked about names for the baby, both male and female. For now, Hogan was the only one who knew, and Cain couldn't wait to find out. "Who are they?" he asked, his voice trembling.

"Lorne."

That was their name for a male. Cain looked down. His lips hurt because he was smiling so widely, but he didn't care. "Welcome to the world, Lorne."

The baby chirped and buried his face against Cain's neck. Cain suspected he was as tired as Cain.

When he looked up, everyone was still staring. Morven's expression was yearning especially, but also a bit scared, and Cain didn't have to ask why. Morven's egg would hatch in only a few weeks, and no one knew what would happen then.

But Morven smiled. "I'm happy for the two of you. I suppose the circumstances weren't the best, but I believe Lorne was born when the two of you most needed him. Congratulations."

"Thank you." Cain's mouth was dry, but there was something he needed to ask. "What happened? Did you catch Caven?"

He knew from Morven's expression that they hadn't even

before Morven shook his head. "He was gone when we arrived. There was only one dragon there, and we arrested him, but he isn't talking."

"The dragon who kidnapped me."

"Exactly. We told him we knew Caven was there and talking to the Eiloren clan, but so far, he's not helping."

"He freed me. Caven ordered him to kill me, but instead, he untied me and told me to run."

Hogan growled at Cain's words, making the baby jerk. Cain wasn't surprised that Hogan's first reaction was to be angry on his behalf or that the second was to reach out and gently rub Lorne's back.

"I see," Morven said. "I'd like to talk to you once you feel better. You're the only one who can tell us what happened."

"We can talk now."

"I don't think so," Hogan intervened. "You need a healer, and so does Lorne. I want to be sure everything is fine with both of you. Once that's done, we're headed home. You can talk to Morven tomorrow. I doubt it's going to change anything."

"What about Caven? Morven needs to arrest him."

Hogan grimaced. He looked at Morven, who shook his head.

"I can't arrest him," Morven explained. "He's the queen's cousin, and he has a lot of support. Not as much as she does, but still. It could become a problem, and the last thing I want is to have a clan war on my hands. We need to be strong against the other clans, not to fight against each other. Besides, I don't think the queen will let me arrest him."

"Why not? He ordered his friend to kill me. He was talking to the Eiloren clan, and they promised to help him take the throne if he gave them me and the egg."

"That's good to know, but I don't think it'll be enough. Hogan is right, though. You need some rest and to see a healer.

We can talk tomorrow, since Caven isn't going anywhere. He's already back at the palace and acting as if nothing happened. He knows we can't do anything to him, and he won't leave. The Ogorth clan is where he has power. He doesn't want to lose it."

Cain wished there was more he could do, but Morven and Hogan were right. He was exhausted and wanted to spend time with his baby and the man he loved.

The others spent a few minutes fawning over Lorne, but the baby was as tired as Cain, and he'd already fallen asleep. Cain was relieved when Hogan guided him through the palace. He could barely keep his eyes open, and it had nothing to do with the beating he'd received.

He wanted to go back to their rooms, but Hogan wouldn't let him until a healer pronounced both him and Lorne healthy enough. By the time that was done, Cain could barely walk, to the point that Hogan had to carry him.

"If I ever have a chance, I'll beat him into the floor," Hogan grumbled as he walked.

"I don't want you to. He doesn't matter."

"He hurt you. You heard the healer."

"I heard her say that I'll be fine."

"And that you would be sore for several days. And that she wants you to rest as much as possible. I don't know why you're standing up for him. He doesn't deserve it."

"He doesn't. But I don't have the energy to focus on him. The only thing I want to focus on is you and Lorne. Everything and everyone else can just disappear. I don't care." He would no doubt change his mind once he felt better, but for now, whatever happened to Caven wasn't his problem. It would be Cain of the future's problem, and that was perfectly fine with him.

Cain was too tired to talk much, so he leaned against Hogan's chest and looked down at Lorne. The baby was perfect and sleeping. He felt like he belonged on Cain's chest, and Cain couldn't get enough of staring at him.

He didn't realize he'd fallen asleep until he felt Hogan lower him. He opened his eyes to see Hogan was putting him down in their nest, and he tried to protest. "I need to clean up. I stink of the forest." And other things like blood, but he didn't want to remind Hogan of that.

"You can clean up tomorrow. We'll have to rearrange the room anyway. I didn't take the time to clean up the mess."

Cain blinked and looked around. Hogan was right—it was a mess. The only thing that was still the same was the nest, but when Cain finally settled in it, he could tell it wasn't the way he'd left it. He was too tired to care, though, and he snuggled deep inside it, holding Lorne to his chest. He felt when Hogan settled with them, and he smiled as he moved closer.

It was perfect. It didn't matter that Cain was sore or that Lorne hadn't been born on the best of days. The three of them were together, a family, and it was all Cain had always wanted.

CHAPTER TEN

Hogan relaxed back in his chair. He'd eaten too much, and he didn't even care that it might slow him down if he had to protect his people. They were gathered in Morven and Sheldon's room, and they were as safe as any of them could be.

Even Blue was there. The queen was over the moon happy that the clan had another baby, and she wanted Lorne and Blue to spend as much time together as they could. The two babies were playing right now, rolling around on the floor, their colors a stark contrast. They were best friends, though, as much as they could considering how young they were and the fact that they were the only two babies in the clan right now.

That wasn't going to last for long. The healers were convinced Morven's egg would hatch any day now, which was why they'd all decided to have dinner here. That way, they could be together while also keeping an eye on the egg. If anything happened, the baby would be born in Morven and Sheldon's rooms, a place where the parents were comfortable.

"You're going to have to roll me back to our rooms," Cain said with a moan.

He was rubbing his stomach, which looked slightly swollen. It was almost as if he were pregnant, and Hogan couldn't help but think about Cain carrying his egg.

He loved Lorne as if he were his son. Lorne *was* his son in every way that mattered. But having a baby had made Hogan wonder if maybe he and Cain could have more of them. He still wasn't comfortable with the thought of carrying an egg, but he supposed he wouldn't mind too much if it was Cain's. It wasn't something they'd talked about, and it was too soon even to bring up the topic. Still, Hogan couldn't wait to see what the future would be like for him and Cain, but also for everyone else.

Morven and Sheldon were about to have a baby. Orran and Blake were happier than ever, although Blake had laughed when Cain had asked him if he and Orran were thinking about having children. As for Octavia and Slavin, as far as Hogan knew, they didn't have anyone special in their lives, but that didn't mean they weren't happy. It would be their turn soon enough, and Hogan would take a lot of pleasure in watching them fall in love. He would make sure to tease them as much as they'd teased him, too.

He couldn't wait.

"Only if you roll me, too," he said.

"How can I do that if you're going to roll me? I shouldn't have eaten so much."

"You needed it." It had been a few weeks, but Cain was still healing from the beating he'd received. Thinking about it angered Hogan, so he did his best not to allow his thoughts to go that way.

Caven was still free and smug. Morven and the queen, as well as most of the clan, knew what he was doing. They also knew why, but he had too much support from the elders. He stoked all the right fires with them—having humans in the clan, and now, welcoming a fugitive from another clan. Eventually, though, those elders would die. Hogan wasn't usually one to wish people would die, but in their case, he did.

Okay, so maybe he *did* wish people would die more often than he should. But those elders were living in the past. They didn't want the clan to change, and that went all the way back to when the queen had taken her father's place. She was a female, but that didn't make her less worthy of being on the throne. The fact that she'd welcomed humans and Cain in the clan was only an excuse Caven and the elders were using. The real problem was that the queen wasn't a male.

"You look like you're going to hit someone," Cain said, peering at Hogan. "You can't blame Sheldon for you eating too much, though."

Hogan frowned. "Do you think I'm going to hit Sheldon?"

"I don't know. You look angry enough."

Hogan shook his head. "I'm not angry." He didn't tell Cain what he'd been thinking about. He didn't want to ruin the evening, and he didn't want either of them to think about Caven tonight. There would be time to worry about him in the weeks and months to come. For now, he and Cain should enjoy themselves.

They had a baby, a family, and friends. What else could anyone want?

"Uh, guys?" Blake said from the corner of the room.

Everyone turned to look at him. He was standing by the nest Sheldon and Morven had made for their egg. He was staring down at it, and when Hogan did the same, he noticed the egg was moving.

He wasn't the only one. Everyone shot to their feet, and it was a scramble to get to the nest. Morven gently took the egg and raised it, turning around so everyone could see it.

"We should probably leave," Cain said.

"Why?" Sheldon asked. He sounded excited but also terrified.

"This is a private moment. I'm sure you and Morven want to be alone when the egg hatches."

Which it was doing right now.

To Hogan's surprise, Sheldon shook his head. "No, please. Stay. Morven and I talked about it, and we'd like you to be here when the baby comes out."

It took Hogan a moment to realize why, and maybe he was wrong, but he didn't think so. Morven and Sheldon were terrified of what their baby would be like. They wanted their friends to be with them to support them in case something went wrong.

Hogan wasn't used to being emotional support to anyone, although he supposed that had changed once Cain had barged into his life. He wanted to stay and be there for Sheldon and Morven, and of course, their baby.

It was alive. The healers had said they were, but Hogan hadn't been able to ignore the niggle of doubt in the back of his mind. What if humans and dragons couldn't have babies together? What if the egg was empty and would never hatch?

He'd been wrong, and he was really fucking relieved he'd been. Because the egg was breaking, and something was obviously pushing against the shell to come out.

Morven moved the egg to his and Sheldon's nest. Everyone else followed them in a tight group, and they all knelt around the nest, ready if anything happened. Even Blue and Lorne came closer, obviously curious about what was happening. They wiggled into the nest, coming to a sitting position by the egg. Neither Morven nor Sheldon pushed them away, so Hogan didn't try to get their attention.

It felt fitting to have them there when the next egg hatched. They would be almost the same age as Morven and Sheldon's child, which hopefully meant they would be friends. They would grow up together, after all.

The egg cracked loudly, making Lorne jump. He looked around until he found Hogan, and when Hogan smiled, he calmed down. His attention moved back to the egg. Hogan was always surprised when he managed to calm down the baby as well as Cain could. He hadn't thought he could do something like that, but he'd been wrong.

"Should we help?" Sheldon asked.

"I'm going to shift so I can communicate with the baby," Morven said. He did just that, taking as little space in the nest as he could so Blue and Lorne didn't have to move away.

With his snout, he gently raised a bit of the shell that had cracked. He let it drop into the nest and peered inside. He reared back, and Hogan felt everyone tense. He did, too, wondering what Morven had seen.

Morven shifted back. "It's incredible," he breathed out.

"What's going on?" Sheldon asked.

There was panic in his voice, but thankfully, Morven grabbed his hand. "Nothing bad. I promise." He reached out and took away another piece of the shell.

Hogan sucked in a breath when he saw what Morven had seen. A small, light green dragon was peering at them. When they saw their group, though, the dragon shifted and became a human baby. Then they saw Blue and Lorne, and they shifted back to their dragon form.

Hogan couldn't believe it. Dragons were always born in their dragon form, and they couldn't shift until they were at least a few years old. Blue never had, and Hogan didn't expect Lorne to be able to anytime soon, either. Morven and Sheldon's baby was different, though. Maybe it was because Sheldon was human, which meant their human side was stronger than it was for normal dragons. Hogan didn't know, and he didn't think anyone did.

Sheldon reached for the baby. They shifted back to their human form, and when Sheldon cradled them to his chest, Hogan saw it was a girl.

Sheldon looked around the room. "Has anyone seen anything like this?"

Hogan shook his head, and he wasn't the only one. Now that he looked closer, when she was in her human form, the baby appeared more human than any other dragon shifter Hogan knew. When she was in her dragon form, though, she was fully dragon.

"She's okay," Morven said. He sounded like he didn't quite believe it. "She's incredible."

"What's her name?" Blake asked. He couldn't seem to look away from Sheldon and the baby.

Sheldon and Morven looked at each other. "Eulalia."

"It's a beautiful name," Cain said.

Eulalia's attention wasn't on her father anymore. She was staring at Blue and Lorne, and she reached for them as if wanting to play. Lorne squeaked, and, to everyone's surprise, Blue shifted.

Hogan was pretty sure his mouth was hanging open, but he couldn't help it. Blue was rolling around in the nest, clearly not knowing how to move as a human. He squawked, then shifted back and glared. Eulalia shifted to her dragon form, too, and jumped out of Sheldon's arms to join the other two babies.

"That wasn't supposed to happen," Blake said.

Slavin snorted. "You can say that. Has he ever shifted before?"

"Not that I know of. His nurses or the queen would have told us if that was the case. I think he just shifted for the first time."

"Well, I guess that having humans here will change a lot of things, certainly more than anyone expected."

Hogan wrapped an arm around Cain. Lorne hadn't shifted, which was mostly a relief. Hogan wasn't ready to deal with a human baby. He suspected that eventually, though, Lorne would try, and that he would succeed. Hogan and Cain had better get used to the idea.

Bringing Sheldon and Blake into the clan wasn't changing just Orran and Morven. They had a bigger influence than anyone could have expected, but Hogan didn't think it was a bad thing. It was the sign that their clan was projecting toward the future rather than the past, which was how it should be.

The three babies rolling around in the nest were the future. One day, Blue would become king. In the meantime, though, Blue was just a baby. He would have time to grow up and take his mother's place, and by the time he did, Hogan hoped the clan would be more welcoming than they were now.

Their family was the best chance to make that happen.

About the Author

Catherine is the creator of several series, most of them paranormal, including the Whitedell Pride Series and the Gillham Pack Series. While she graduated in translation, she decided to go the writer's way because it was more fun to create her own stories and characters.

She's been living in Italy for more than twenty years, but she's a daughter of the North—Belgium to be precise—and she misses it so much that she's already planning to move back.

She loves pizza—probably too much—her son, her pets, and of course, books. She sneaks some reading time into her schedule every time she has five minutes free from writing, demands from her various pets and son, and lastly, housework.

Connect with her:

lievens.catherine@gmail.com
BookBub: https://www.bookbub.com/authors/catherine-lievens
Website: https://authorcatherinelievens.com/
Facebook: https://www.facebook.com/catherine.lievens.9
Facebook Group: https://www.facebook.com/groups/411788002341528/
Twitter: https://twitter.com/authorCLievens
Newsletter: https://authorcatherinelievens.com/newsletter/

www.ingramcontent.com/pod-product-compliance
Lightning Source LLC
LaVergne TN
LVHW020626100826
845148LV00012B/2067